Infatuated with a Real One

Loyalty

D1550776

Infatuated with a Real One

Caught Up With A Street Nigga

Ain't nothing harder than loving a thug

Always dodging the cops, fearful that your man could end up dead or in jail.

This life feels worse than hell.

I can't believe things ended up this way,

But then again, I had a type from day one.

I love the way he wears fitted hats, the way his pants hang low,

All the money he has that I can spend, but I hate laying low.

I hate having to watch my back every minute, every second of each day

It's so hard to let him go because my love continues to grow in every way.

He is a thug, but he's my thug

I'm always getting judged by my family or his.

Judged by people who don't know me from a can of paint

But I continue to hold him down like the anchor in the sea

And hope that someday he will change, even if he ain't.

He is a real nigga, but he is my real nigga

I hate being in the middle of shootouts

Having to stick drugs up my womanhood whenever we get pulled over by the cops

The fast life is tempting when you're looking from afar and you see the fast money, the fancy cars with the drop tops

When you're in love with a thug,

Striving

I strive to become better than I was yesterday

Although I don't know what my future may hold

My choices are a reflection on how I think

And my success just proves that I'm bold

I dreamed of standing by a river last night

Trying to reflect, but I seemed confused

I was extremely tired of rejection

And the feelings of being abused and used

I woke up another day, which means another chance

To truly fight for all of my dreams

I strive, I push, and I will not give up

Although succeeding is harder than it seems

I felt my growth, and it was a scary feeling

But I couldn't stop right there

I had to change and get rid of some things

And eliminate the people who didn't care

I was lied on and mistreated

There were days I couldn't afford to pay my bills

I didn't realize those things were all distractions

But I did realize that stress kills

I let go, and I stepped out with a mind filled with faith

With a heart that is made of gold

I strive to feel accomplished and to be a provider

Now I'm excited about what my future may hold.

Text Shan to 22828 to stay up to date with new releases, sneak peeks, contest, and more...

Check your spam if you don't receive an email thanking you for signing up.

Text SPROMANCE to 22828 to stay up to date on new releases, plus get information on contest, sneak peeks, and more!

I would like to thank my family members for being there along the way. I truly miss my grandparents in Heaven, and I cherished the time I had with them while they were here with us on Earth. Thanks to my oldest son for pitching his ideas about how much I need to write and how to grab a reader's attention. Thanks to my readers for supporting me and reading all of my work. Thanks for the art of storytelling and to be able to share what I'm thinking with so many people. I am truly thankful for my publishing home and my pen sisters for motivating me and for us being able to work as a team. Thank you to the whole Shan Presents movement because this company is really the best. Thanks to all of my children for being my inspiration of why I do everything that I do. I write to provide for them, to make sure they have everything they need, because that's what we do as mothers. Thanks to everyone for the reviews that you leave; the feedback helps me better myself with everything I do. Special shout outs to my brother and uncles, who are also writers, with unique gifts. Thanks to my auntie for being someone who listens to me, and attempt to understand me, because I can be a complicated human being.

I hope you all enjoy this novel, and there will be more acknowledgments at the end of this book. So, if you think I have forgotten about you, I truly haven't.

Table of Contents

Chapter 1: Good Girl Doing Bad Shit

Legacy

I am Legacy Hayes. A star I was born, and a star I will always be. That is what my grandmother used to tell me. When I was little, I was always profiled as the good girl. Being the good girl had so much pressure to it; you can't smoke, and you can't drink. Staying out late is prohibited and going to clubs is out of line. I couldn't hold the weight of being a good girl because of my low self-esteem and my unhappiness that I carried deep inside.

At the age of thirteen, I was having sex, and by the age of fifteen, I was fighting and running the streets. I got pregnant with my first child at the age of sixteen. Little did I know, my deep love for my daughter wasn't going to be enough to help me keep her with me. Staying with other people can be hectic, and staying with your parents can sometimes be worse than staying with a stranger that you barely know. Because of that, I lost my child to the system.

At first, when Social Services was called, I was given an African American social worker. She told me that she would do everything in her power to help me keep my baby, like job searching and getting me into a program that would take my daughter and I in, because living with my mother wasn't suitable enough. You see, my mother argued a lot about everything, because she was either high or drunk. And when I had my daughter, our next-door neighbors knew I had a newborn child, so they called the police to our house, and they claimed my baby might have been in danger.

Maybe they were right. There was nothing in this world that was worse than picking up crack pipes lying around the house or beer bottles that were halfway empty with cigarette butts inside of them. I was dealing with a mother who was a drug addict, a drunk, and who spent her money on ridiculous shit. After I had my daughter, I craved for change because there was nothing that I wanted to do more than be the kind of mother that my daughter needed me to be. The kind of mother that my own mother wasn't.

I blamed my mother for that for so many years and so did a lot of other people. I felt like she could have been a better mother and not fuss and fight with me all of the time, knowing that I had a newborn child in her home. Other people blamed her because she was the type of person who didn't allow other people to get in the middle of situations that were going on between her and her children. I simply thought that was wrong because there comes a time when other people need to interfere for the sake of the child when it comes to a certain kind of parent. She always got mad when I called her out on her shit, always got angry when I tried to help her get her shit together. By the time I had my daughter, it had been years of me seeing my mother like that. She thought I was stupid, but I knew what a crack head looked like before I saw a damn pipe. We came from the hood, and crack heads were all over the projects. Her drugs were the reason I ran away at such a young age. Her drugs and behavior are the very reasons my life has been fucked up the way it has been.

Everything spiraled downhill within a blink of an eye, and although I was hurt beyond measure, I was focused on getting my daughter back. I was showing up to all of my visitation dates to see my baby girl, London. I shed so many tears that, each time I left visitation, my eyes were damn near swollen. My baby cried for me every time I left her, and there was nothing I could do. That's a hurtful feeling, you know; to have the only good thing in your life, the only person who depends on you and who you depend on for unconditional love, ripped right out of your arms and living with someone else. To see my baby cry like that, every time I had to hand her over to strangers when my few hours of visitation time was up. To walk out of that same building that I had to be at every Tuesday and Thursday and see my baby stare at me and cry as she was placed in the car seat of a social worker's car.

I did a lot of job searching, catching the city bus every day, trying to find a job. I can't even count how much money I spent doing applications for two bedroom apartments, so my baby girl would have a suitable place to come home to. The moment my social worker was changed from an African American woman to a Caucasian woman wasn't nearly the problem. The problem was that the Caucasian social worker seemed pretty suspect, having me sign documentation that I was too young to understand. My daughter had been staying with my aunt, and the moment I signed that unfamiliar documentation, that social worker went over to my aunt's home and took my daughter away from her as my aunt cried, begging her not to.

To make matters worse, there was a family, a Caucasian woman and an African-American male, who were in court trying to adopt my daughter a week after that. I fought and cried on that stand to get custody of my daughter, and the last thing I remember the judge saying was, "Well, you stayed in trouble years ago and were in and out of juvenile. I think this is no different. Besides, you will always have more children."

Those words made my heart stop because I was being judged by things I had done years prior, and when I walked out of the courtroom, I overheard the Caucasian social worker telling the parents, who were trying to adopt my daughter, that it would be over soon. I did everything I was told to do. I looked for a job, I completed counseling, I went to parenting classes, I was hired at the Waffle House and was working, and I moved out of my mother's house and in with a friend, who had extra space, until I found my own place. I even stayed away from my aunt's home because they told me that my daughter could be there as long as I didn't go over there until the court process was over with.

3

Somehow, I can't seem to get that out of my head; that day replays in my head before I go to bed at night and when I awake each morning. I was lied to by a social worker, and nothing was ever done about it. She went to the courts and tried to help the foster family instead of me. I later found out that the foster mother, who fought so hard to get my baby, couldn't have children of her own. The foster father was a loan officer at a bank and made really good money. I started wondering if they paid the social worker off to help the case go in their favor. I was only seventeen years old, and I lost my first child in the most fucked up way.

After that, I stopped giving a fuck about any and everything. I wasn't always that way. Coming from a broken home, having the kind of mother that I had and a father that was in prison, was a lot for a teenager to endure. My grandmother passed away while I was young, and that had a major impact on my life. She was the only good thing in my life. She made me happy, and because I left home, I wasn't even able to make it to her funeral. My mother not only did drugs but she sold them for a living as well.

My father, Yankee, was a big time drug dealer, and everyone knew him on the streets. People were often afraid to fuck with me when they found out who my father was. He was doing life in prison, and I just knew I would never see him again. You would think I would get a simple phone call from him, but that didn't happen either. I guess that's how I turned out to be who I am, doing the things I do. I didn't know what love was or how to be loved by a man. I had no moral support system. When I was younger, my mother had a major effect on the people around me. Nobody wanted to take me in because they were too afraid that my mother would show up at their doorstep, trying to fight them.

It was no different when I had my daughter, so for that reason alone, I hated the fact she was even my mother. My life had played out like a ripple effect. My mother was the main reason everything in my life had gone wrong, why people didn't want to be around me, and why I had lost my child. Why the judge judged me about my past because, if it weren't for her, I would have never been running away or being rebellious in the first place.

After I lost my daughter, I stayed in Charlotte, North Carolina and was living pretty much from hotel to hotel by the age of seventeen. It was better than staying with my mother, and although I blamed her for the events that had occurred, she was still my mother, so I respected her, and I visited from time to time. I grew out of being insecure and having low self-esteem, and I started looking at myself in the mirror. I realized that I was beyond beautiful, so that began to get to my head a little.

I had a body that was shaped like a coca cola bottle, with a caramel brown skin complexion and some catty eyes that were slanted. I was standing at five seven and was able to get whatever I wanted with my looks, my shape, and a fake identification card. The men, who checked me into hotels, didn't even look at the face on my identification card because they were too busy staring at my ass in the short ass shorts that I wore with my ass cheeks sticking out.

"Yes, I need a room." I handed the front desk associate the fake identification card. My beautiful, C-cup breasts were always a distraction, so I made sure to wear the proper clothing that would show my breasts and the rest of my body.

I hung out with a few girls, but I was so conceited that I didn't think any of them had shit on me. But these girls were my bitches, and I did everything with them. Well, I had a line of niggas that I was fucking with, and none of them were anything I would get serious with. Everything that I was doing was to feel numb; I didn't want to feel the pain anymore. I had lost all hope of getting my daughter back. I had no support system and no strong foundation with a line of people standing behind me, waiting there to catch me when I fell.

This day was different because I met the most handsome, butter pecan, brown skinned man a woman could view. I was a fool for men that were from Atlanta, Georgia because I loved their slang that was often very impossible to imitate.

His name was Vonne, and I had grown close to him. He knew about my daughter, London, because he was the first person I had opened up to after she was taken. Being with him, I didn't fight so hard to feel numb because he made me feel hope. He often talked about helping me get London back and us all being together. I cried on his chest many times, and we stared at London's photos together, admiring her beauty because she was the spitting image of me.

That's what attracted me to him the most. I went from staying from hotel to hotel, to being at his apartment all of the time. Things were moving pretty fast between us, and it was like the most advanced puppy love a couple could experience. I didn't have any guy friends anymore because I cut them all off to give him a fair chance. I wasn't sure if he was worth it, but there was something about him that made me want to find out. Vonne was brown skinned as well, with some small, but gorgeous, eyes. He was skinny as hell, and he wore cornrows in his head. I couldn't wait to catch the bus and get to him every day. I had managed to pick up a job at the Waffle House, waiting tables, and he didn't stay that far from my workplace. Each day, I got on the bus, rode it for two minutes, and I was already in front of his apartment complex. I took a change of clothes and a bag with my body oil and makeup always, because I didn't want him seeing me in my work clothes all of the time, nor smelling waffles and bacon on my body. I wanted to look like something, each and every time I approached his doorstep.

Knock. Knock. Knock.

I stood there, trying to look sexy, while waiting for someone to answer the door. I wore some tight blue jeans, with a half shirt, and some sandals to show off my pretty toes, which I kept done. My hair was cut short, and I had my belly and tongue pierced.

"Hey, you can come on in. Vonne is in the shower," his roommate said as he stood in the doorway. I stood there, chewing some bubble gum so my breath wouldn't reek of cigarette smoke. I had smoked as soon as I got off the bus, and Vonne didn't smoke cigarettes.

"Okay. I will go in his room and surprise him when he gets out." I walked right past his roommate, letting him know that I had accepted his invitation to come inside.

One of the things that I hated about the situation was that he had roommates. I was picky in so many ways, and I preferred my niggas with their own everything. But if they had a good heart and was about something, I was willing to make an exception. Besides the fact that he did share an apartment with two other men, he had a really good job working for Merita Bakery, and I was willing to work with that. I couldn't knock a man for trying, regardless of his line of work and hustle.

I stepped foot into his small bedroom and took off all of my clothes as I heard the water from the shower stop and saw the steam coming from the bathroom door. I laid there on his small bed with my matching blue panties and bra on. The bathroom door slowly opened, and he jumped because he wasn't expecting me. He stood there with only a white towel wrapped around his wet body as I opened my legs, giving him a sexy invitation to come closer.

"Damn, baby; you scared me. I didn't know you were coming. How did you get in?" Vonne asked as he looked at me while he took the towel off his waist to dry the rest of his body.

"Your roommate let me in, and plus, I wanted to surprise you," I said while putting my legs high in the sky.

"Damn, baby; you look good, and you smell good as hell. What's that fragrance you're wearing?" He approached my sexy body, and he sniffed me and kissed me like he was ready to lick off every bit of the fragrance I was wearing.

"It's a body oil called *Sex on the Beach*." That was one of my favorites. I always loved to buy those oils out of the hair supply store, along with the lip-gloss. The oils were five dollars per bottle but always had me smelling like a million bucks.

He pulled out his dick, and although it was small, I worked with it as much as I could. The way he ate my pussy was something else though. He had my legs quivering, and he sucked every ounce of the *Sex on the Beach* body oil fragrance off my body as well. By the time we were finished, all he wanted to do was cuddle and hold me close. He loved to speak on his dreams for the future, and I loved that about him as well.

"One day, I want to move you back to Georgia and have some babies - after we get London back." He looked me directly in my eyes, indicating that he was very serious about a future with me.

"Damn, but what will we do there? I mean, it sounds like a good idea, just being able to start over somewhere else period. It is a great idea." I tried not to stare back into his eyes. I was still in the stage of trying to hold back a little. I really liked Vonne, but I wasn't in love with him yet. The fact that I could tell him everything was definitely a plus, but I still wasn't sure if he was the one for me yet.

"I guess I could transfer with my job or possibly take a manager's position at KFC or something." Vonne shared his dreams with me, and his dreams weren't what I expected. I hoped he wanted a little more out of life than what he did. I had never heard of anyone wanting to settle for a job at a fast food restaurant or any restaurant period. Hell, I was tired of working for the Waffle House, but I had to make some kind of legitimate money.

"You don't want much, and it can happen as long as I know you will love me and protect me always." I hugged him and gave him a kiss. Although his dreams weren't the dreams that made someone rich, I ultimately wanted someone who could make me feel secure and safe. I would never settle and have children with someone who wasn't willing to put his life on the line for his family. Most of all, I needed the man that I chose to spend forever with to always put me first.

We lay there for a little while longer, and then, we got up and got dressed. We had to go our separate ways but not before he treated me to some Baskin Robbins ice cream. Our relationship was perfect for some time. We spent our time doing the usual things that couples engaged in, like going out to eat together, going to the movies, or simply just ordering movies off of Netflix at home. He moved from that small apartment into a big house in a middle class neighborhood - with his roommates of course. After that, things turned left right before our eyes because his roommates always threw big ass parties, and they acted as if they didn't want me to come over that much anymore.

One day, I was lying in his bed because I had spent the night, and I was off of work for a few days. I wanted to spend those days with him because it wasn't often that we were given the same days off of work. His roommate came bursting in the door, without knocking, and was blatantly disrespectful, having outbursts like a five-year-old child having a tantrum.

"You've got to get the fuck out of here!" His roommate was obviously angry, but I didn't know why, so I looked at him with a look of confusion at first.

"Yo, chill out. Who are you talking about?" Vonne stood up as if he was trying to calm down his so-called friend.

"I'm talking about your bitch. She's got to go." His roommate stared at me while pointing his fingers into my direction.

"Who the fuck are you calling a bitch?" I got up because it wasn't nothing for me to swing on a man. I was gangsta, and I was about to show him what the fuck I was made of.

9

"I'm talking to your ass!" he stated. He stood in the doorway of the room and continued to be disrespectful."

"I'm calling my mom, and then I'm leaving." I pulled out my phone to call my mother to come and pick me up because I wasn't dealing with that shit. She was only right down the street, a few minutes away. No matter what I went through with my mother, she was there for me if I needed her. When it came down to anyone trying to harm me in any kind of way, she was there, fighting my battles as well. Maybe she felt guilty and that was her way of trying to make things better, even though it wouldn't because I still didn't have London.

The worst part was that I felt like Vonne wasn't taking up for me like he was supposed to. Hell, he was paying half of the rent, and his roommate wanted me to pay a portion as well. Fuck out of here with the bullshit because that was some square ass shit. I needed a man who could complete me, a man who would defend me with his own life. I needed a man who made me feel whole, complete, and most of all, safe. I didn't feel safe in that very moment. I wasn't scared at all, but I should have felt like my boyfriend was defending me at that very moment. If I couldn't call him a protector, then why in the hell would I call him a husband? My heart was beating faster than it normally would be, my eyes were turning red, and tears began running down my face. It was like clockwork. Whenever I grew angry, I began to cry right before I lost it. I felt sorry for people who took my tears as a sign of weakness because anyone who knew me knew that when I started crying, and my eyes were bloodshot red, then that meant to run like hell and don't look back.

"Man, that's messed up. I pay half of the rent, and you're telling my girl she's got to leave." Vonne looked him dead in his eyes, and I could tell, as he was standing there, that he was almost afraid to stand up for himself and for me.

"Hell yeah, unless she comes up with some money to pay rent, too." His roommate acted like he wanted to get in my face, but Vonne blocked the path and was the only thing in the way of this rude ass, so-called man laying his hands on me.

"I've got money, but I bet your disrespectful, bitch ass ain't getting a damn thing from me." I walked towards the door and opened it so that I could leave, and I saw my mother and stepfather coming right down the street to pick me up.

"Baby, come whoop her ass." He told his tall, fat, girlfriend, who was Caucasian, to try and fight me. He was Caucasian as well and was good looking, but his bitch looked like a bag of shit. She walked towards me, and she thought she had a chance; maybe because I was much smaller than her, but the bitch had me fucked up. She swung on me and missed, and I pulled her by the hair and dragged that bitch right outside on the porch as my mother pulled over and jumped out the car with my stepfather.

"Oh, hell no. It's go time, bitch!" Yes, my mother, Renee, was gangsta too, always fighting bitches and niggas and winning every fight she got into. She had hands that would make a bitch piss in her very own pants because they always thought that they were about that life until my mother came up and stole off on their asses.

My mother was a light skinned bombshell with slanted eyes, just like me. I got my looks from her but my skin color from my father. My stepfather was Hispanic, and he was a good man because he put up with my mother. She was definitely hell on wheels.

I had the bitch and was whooping her ass on my own, but my mother jumped in the fight anyway. So, yes, we jumped that bitch. After my mother and I finished, we just walked away from that house, cursing those bitches out. I knew Vonne and I were finished. Not because he wanted it to end, but because I didn't feel protected. I always knew, in my heart, that when I found a man who would protect me, with his words and actions, then he would be the one.

I went to stay with my mother for a while, attempting to slow down a little because I didn't want to experience any shit like that again. That's definitely how I became the bitch who would fuck a nigga and leave his place before sunrise. Niggas loved that shit and found it attractive, so I had plenty of ballers blowing up my phone because I went for the niggas with money and shit to offer. You know who they are - the niggas with nice ass cars, rims, a pocketful of money with rubber bands wrapped around it, and with their own fucking houses and condos.

Vonne wouldn't stop blowing my phone up, crying and shit, but I was done with that chapter of my life and surely onto the next. Maybe I was searching for something perfect, or maybe he was too good to be true the whole entire time. Regardless of the situation, I couldn't be with him unless he was tough. Surely, I was a strong girl, but that was the weakest point of my life, and I needed a man who had enough strength for the both of us.

The texts wouldn't stop coming, and so, I knew what Vonne planned on doing. He texted me and told me that he was leaving North Carolina and moving back to Georgia. He said that, if it was truly meant to be, he would bump back into me one day, and we could go from there. He said that he wasn't giving up on me because I was the love of his life. I read those messages, and yet, I still wasn't convinced that I should take him back. It was like I was growing to be a cold-hearted individual because I was still hurting. That was the moment when everything started weighing down on me. You know, when you start thinking about everything and how overwhelming your life had become.

I broke down really bad to the point where you would have thought that my tears would have formed a puddle of water. I was confused in so many ways, and I couldn't see the light at the end of the tunnel. Something good had to happen for me, or I was going to give up completely. My intentions were never to hurt Vonne, but I was so broken that there was a lot of inner fixing that I needed badly. That was the type of woman I was becoming; I was willing to let people go before they walked out of my life. I never had anything consistent for myself, and it was showing in so many ways. I wasn't mentally nor physically stable, and I needed a love that could make me feel something better than what I had been feeling. I needed a love that would take away all of the pain. I needed a love that would ultimately make me feel safe and secure. Vonne was a pretty decent guy, and I was sure that he would meet someone, who was a better match for him, but I wasn't that girl.

Chapter 2: Crossing Paths With a Real Nigga

Legacy

I was walking down the street, on the west side, when he stopped his car in the middle of the street. He drove a gray, newer model Mustang, and he was handsome. He was light skinned, and just from looking at his fitted hat and the expensive outfit he had to match it, I could tell he wore the best of clothes. He was well groomed, and his smell was addictive. I could smell him from standing in front of the passenger's seat window. As the window rolled down, I bent over, showing him my flawless smile.

"What's up? Where are you going?" Staring at my breasts, he asked me where I was heading as he gave me the sexiest look a nigga could give.

"I'm just taking a walk to the store." As I let him know exactly where I was heading to, I looked at him with my thick lip-gloss on my full lips and black eyeliner under my gorgeous, slanted eyes

"What's your name, beautiful?" He looked dead at me as he showed interest in finding out about me. With his hands on the wheel and his feet on the brakes, I knew that he was in a rush to get somewhere; he didn't even bother putting the car in park.

"My name is Legacy, and what is your name?" I asked as the heels I wore started hurting my feet. I started to wonder what the hell I was thinking about, making them my choice of shoes to walk down the street in.

"My name is Skrilla," he said as he took a sip of a clear liquid that was in a foam, white cup. As I looked on the seat, he had a bottle of

Cîroc, so I knew he only drank the best. Now, I knew two things about him. He had money, and he was picky about everything he did. It's funny how a girl can scope out things about a nigga after only a few minutes of conversation.

"I know that's not your name. What's your real name?" I was positive that he gave me his street name, but that's not what I needed from him.

"Come and roll with me, and I will tell you everything you need to know about me," he said as he insisted that I get into his gray Mustang.

"Okay," I said as I looked at his sexy ass. I was skeptical about leaving with this man; I didn't know him from a can of paint. For all I knew, he could have been a murderer. Truth be told, after losing my daughter, I became a little more reckless with my lifestyle. I was here and there and didn't know if I was coming or going. I didn't know if I wanted to do the right thing, keep my job, and work on getting my shit together or if I wanted to get high and live the party lifestyle. Losing a child that you didn't want to lose, in an unfair manner, can change your whole life and your opinions about life for that matter. At some point, I said fuck it and decided to see what this man was all about.

I got into his car because I wasn't down for walking while catching a horrible cramp in my legs because of the clear stilettos I sported. As I got into the car, I pulled my dark blue jean dress down and placed my hair into a ponytail. It was really hot outside, and it felt good for me to feel the air blowing across my face because of the air conditioner from his car.

It was May and indeed the wrong time for me to have a quick weave in my hair. I needed something different and was absolutely tired of the short, natural hairstyle that was actually beautiful on me. I was actually a hair stylist, and I did hair to make extra money on the side from time to time. Being a hair stylist saved me tons of money because I was able to do my own as well.

Skrilla was charming but hood, and I could tell that he was a ladies' man. I'm a pretty complicated girl, and I could tell that he was complicated and hard to figure out as well. We detoured and prolonged going to the store because he said he was hungry. He took me to his favorite spot, which was Chili's Bar and Grill. We both ordered the triple dipper platter, and then, he stopped by the gas station.

"Is there anything you want out of here?" Skrilla asked. I knew he was the type of guy who would spoil me and get me anything I wanted, so I grasped that quickly.

"Yes, a pack of Newport's and a Smirnoff, please," I replied in the sweetest way possible.

He came back from the gas station, and he had everything I asked him to get plus some cigars, which let me know that he got high too. We pulled up at the Courtyard Hotel, and I knew I had to be something special. This hotel was going to cost him $129 per night, and that was before taxes. I had met so many niggas in the past who thought that they were doing something by taking their women to Motel 6, paying forty dollars a night, and some of these hoes actually went for that shit. He went inside the office to pay for the room, while I waited on him in the car. As soon as he came out, he came and got me out the car and took me into the hotel room that he paid for. I was nervous as hell; it's nothing like the first night, and I wasn't really sure what was going to happen between us. I didn't plan on doing anything; I just wanted to allow chemistry and the right timing to take its place.

We sat on the queen-sized bed, in the comfortable room, and he placed the food down so that he could roll up a blunt.

"Do you smoke?" Skrilla asked as he licked the swisher cigar before splitting it wide open.

"Yes, I do, but I'm hungry as hell too." I opened the plate of food and started dipping the southwestern egg rolls into the honey mustard and ranch. I took a bite while I slid off the uncomfortable high heels.

"Damn, you look sexy as hell." He stared at me while he put his weed into the cigar, rolled it up, and then licked it to make sure it would stay closed. He had the sexiest lips, and all I wanted to do was kiss him, although his compliment had made me nervous all over again. I wanted to do something to break the ice even more, and that's when I had the bright idea to go swimming.

"Just follow me. I want to do something spontaneous," I suggested as he got up and followed. He grabbed a towel, knowing I would need one, and we went directly to the pool. I had always loved to swim since a young age. The way I learned was crazy. Someone pushed me into a swimming pool, and they told me I could either swim or die. It was almost like the people in my life had a fucked up way of showing me they cared about me.

In a sexy manner, I took my clothes off, only leaving on my bra and panties, and then I jumped into the swimming pool. My hair was wet and all, but I didn't care about that. He sat in one of the chairs and smoked his blunt, while he stared at me swimming in the pool. It was late, around eleven o'clock, so surely nobody was supposed to be there, but we were going to break the rules that night. As I turned around and looked, he was putting his blunt out, and security was walking up on us.

The security flashed his flashlight and told us that we would have to leave, so I got out of the pool, and he came towards me and gently placed the towel around my wet body. He then grabbed me by my waist, and we went back into the room.

"Damn, that was a close call." Skrilla looked nervous. He thought the security guard was approaching us concerning the smell of the weed. From the looks of things, I could tell he didn't have time to get arrested, and neither did I.

"I know; I'm so glad that he did not smell your weed. Overall, it was fun swimming this late; the water felt amazing." I wanted him to know that the night was still young, and I was having the time of my life. As I dried my body with the towel, that was now wet as well, I reached for the blunt he had rolled on the dresser. Picking up the blunt, I could tell that it was some of the best weed I had smoked in a while, Then, I cracked open my Smirnoff to get my throat wet a little. He had his Ciroc, and I cracked that open and started chugging his bottle as well. Everything became a blur, and I was pretty much faded at that point.

I sat on the bed beside him, and we spent the next hour talking about everything. It's funny how you meet someone, and instantly you've bonded with them, as if you have known them your whole life. That's what happened between us.

"I think you're special," he said as he started nibbling on my ear. He didn't really have to tell me that because that is how he made me feel. It started to rain outside, and that really set the mood. There was something about the rain that made me feel some type of way. I began to grow horny as I saw his penis stand up through the pants he had on while he stared at me. It seemed to me like he was waiting for the right moment to make his move, but I wanted this man. I didn't give a damn if it was too early because I damn sure was about to make my move. I started rubbing on his hard dick through his pants, and when he licked his lips and put his cup of Cîroc down, I knew it was time to see what he was like in bed.

He pulled my underwear down and reached for the magnum condom that he had placed on the nightstand. Obviously he knew he was going to get some because the pack of condoms was fresh and had never been opened. I was attracted to the fact that he practiced safe sex because I didn't want to have any more kids, especially after all I had been through. He took off his clothes – his shoes, his shirt, and finally his pants. His body smelled differently than his clothes did. Although he didn't have on any cologne, I could tell that he must have washed his clothes in the detergent *Gain*. He smelled like he bathed in lavender body gel, and I loved to sniff him, just to take in the full effect of the scent.

He placed the condom on his dick after taking off his green, Tommy Hilfiger boxers, and then, he pulled my waist, and I got on top of him. The way I rode his dick let him know I was a winner. He moaned, and no matter how hard I tried to hold my feelings back, I couldn't. While he penetrated me with his nine-inch dick, my walls felt every bit of it, and I was fully pleased. He was different, and that attracted every inch of my caramel body. His dick was so good that I had to remind myself that I wasn't allowed to catch feelings, not this early. There's nothing sexier than a man who knows how to work every inch of your body and has the perfect size equipment to follow behind the strokes.

"Damn, baby. This shit feels so good." Skrilla moaned and grabbed my plump ass. He loved what he was feeling, and I could tell by his body language. He sucked on my neck, and I didn't care if marks would appear because I loved the way he felt too. He was rough with me, the type to smack my ass and grab my thighs tightly, but I enjoyed every bit. He kept placing my body in different positions, to feel my wet walls in many different ways. He sucked on every inch of my body, including my toes and the crack of my ass. I never had anyone to suck on the crack of my ass, and then, he licked his lips just like he had sucked on a spoon after dipping it in some butter pecan ice cream.

His body began to shake as mine trembled, and I could feel the cum squirt from his dick inside of me. I was scared as hell because I knew we were using protection, and I couldn't understand why I was feeling this warm cum all inside of me.

I had come so many times, and although my body was on fire, I was only worried about the one time he had come and where exactly he came at. I got up to turn on the light, just to see why I felt the warm cum run down my thighs out of my pussy. I looked for the condom while he laid in the bed, and it wasn't on his dick. I went into the bathroom to check myself and pulled the condom out of my pussy. It was clear that it had burst, and there was cum all inside of me.

"Oh my God; how in the hell did this happen?" I was panicking like hell. I couldn't help but wonder if he had some type of disease and if all of this was worth it on the first night. The scariest feeling was thinking, *'What if he has AIDS or some shit?'* because I knew I would truly be fucked.

"Shit, baby. You ain't got nothing to worry about; I'm clean." Skrilla was nervous that I would remain upset; maybe because he didn't want that night to be the last time he would have me. He wanted this thing we had just experienced to turn into something far more. I knew I had some good pussy, and I knew he'd be hooked after feeling all of me the way he did.

"I guess I have no choice but to take your word." I went and put my clothes back on and told him I was ready to go. I was upset, but there wasn't anything I could do at that point except to wait it out and hope that I didn't catch anything. I would definitely have to follow up with my doctor and have them run some tests. It wouldn't take them long to tell me something.

"Why do you want to leave? The room is already paid for and shit." He looked hopeful and tried to convince me that I should stay with him for the whole night. He sat up, put his t-shirt back on, and looked sad. I could tell that the hoes who he fucked with were so sprung that they took pride in laying up with him. But I was a different kind of girl, and I did shit my way.

"I'd rather go home and sleep in my own bed," I said as I brushed my hair back down in place and placed my belongings back into my purse. I liked him too much for it to be the first night, but I was never the type of girl who was interested in moving too fast. I wanted to wait it out and see where things would go because you always have to give a tiger his chance to reveal his true stripes, before jumping off the deep in.

Skrilla got up and dropped me off at home. He looked disappointed, but hell, I was upset that the condom had burst like that. As soon as I stepped foot into the apartment, I headed straight for the shower to clean my body and douche my pussy - just in case. Even if he didn't have anything, I didn't want to take the chance of getting pregnant either because I wasn't on any type of birth control. I went to sleep in my t-shirt with him deep on my mind, and no matter how hard I tried to stop thinking about him, it was impossible.

I fell asleep with my cellphone on vibrate, and when I woke up the next morning, I had four missed calls from him. I didn't call him back because I wanted him, and I truly felt like the way to get him was to ignore him. I know how stupid it sounds, but in some cases, it works when a man really wants you because he will go out of his way to get your attention and make you feel extra special.

I went that whole week, ignoring him, and then, he showed up where he knew I would be. I was standing outside at my friend's house, and there he was. He pulled up, placed the car in park on the side of the road, and he had only one thing on his mind. I could tell by staring him dead into his brown eyes that he had been thinking of me endlessly as well.

"Where are you going?" he asked, and I knew exactly what he wanted to hear, so I quickly gave him a response.

"I'm going with you," I said as I hopped into the car and kissed him on his lips. It was at that very moment in which I thought I was falling in love with this man.

That was the second night that I was with him, although I had waited for a whole week, and I was shocked to see we had pulled up at his father's home. We both went inside, and I was nervous about meeting his father because I had on some revealing shorts and a half top. I looked like a hooker, and that was no way to meet someone's parent. Surprisingly, his father was nice and didn't look judgmental; I should have known there was a reason for that. I didn't bother to think of the reasons why his father was so accepting of me that quickly. I just wanted to be around him. All the questions that a girl should be asking right away were all the questions that I put on the backburner. The only thing I was worried about at that point was finding out this man's real name and what turned him on in a woman.

"What is your real name? I know Skrilla isn't what your mother named you," I asked while placing my hands on his face as we sat in his car, listening to Jeezy.

"My name is Sydney Black," he stated as he reached for his license to prove that was his real name.

I looked at his license. I knew this man had told me he was twenty-eight; hell, he knew I was only eighteen years old. I had just had a birthday a few months prior on May 16th, and here it was July 4th. His birthday was July 11th, only a week away, and I thought he was turning twenty-nine. That was the first moment in our relationship that I felt a little stupid.

"Baby, if I would have told you that I'm thirty-two years old, you wouldn't have given me the time of the day. I need you, Legacy, and I don't want to lose you." He kissed me with the softest kiss on my lips, and I was instantly drawn back into his spell. I was head over hills for him, and that feeling couldn't be taken away that easily.

If looks could tell everything, they'd say he was only twenty-eight because he looked extremely good for his age. He took care of himself very well and only used the best products and expensive soaps and lotions on his skin. He didn't eat pork, and he was a very picky eater period. His smell was off the charts, and he was clean. He kept his car and wherever he laid his head clean, but I ran into the same problem with him that I experienced with Vonne. He didn't have his own place;

he stayed with his mother. He said that he had broken up with his ex-girlfriend, and he let her have the house because she had his baby and didn't have anywhere else to go. He was my man, so I believed him.

We spent our days going out to eat and shopping. He would take me to Foot Locker and buy me Jordan's and Air Forces. That's all that he wore, so he wanted me to wear the same. He would take me to the best restaurants to eat at - Red Lobster, Chili's Bar and Grill, Applebee's, and Ruby Tuesdays. Anything that my heart desired but with class. Our nights were spent smoking fat blunts of the best weed and having steamy, great sex. We were no longer using protection, and I felt more bonded with this man than I had ever felt with any other man I had dated up until that point of my life. I never stepped back to ask myself whether or not we were moving too fast; I enjoyed whatever it was that we had going on. I tried to hold it in, but after a month of dating, I couldn't help it. Those important words slipped out of my mouth.

"I love you." I stopped myself in my own tracks, afraid that he wouldn't feel the same way. His lips moved, and I was surprised because I expected him to not say anything back. It was too early.

"I love you, too; I don't know what it is, but I fell in love with you, Legacy." He looked me straight in my eyes and told me he felt the same way. I was so happy, and at that moment, I felt like he was the one for me. I tilted my head, unzipped his pants, and sucked his dick like a champion in his car. My head was bomb, but I knew my pussy was way better. I pulled off my shorts, got on top of him, and rode him right there in the car. My pussy was so good to him that he came within the first five minutes of me riding him.

"Damn, baby; look what you've done to me," he said as he came all inside of me. I leaned over and put my tongue in his mouth as his dick stayed inside of me.

"You were incredible, babe." I licked my lips as I prepared to go down on him and lick the drippings of whatever cum that he didn't inject in my pussy. I twirled my tongue around his dick and then deep throated the whole thing. His eyes rolled to the back of his head as he enjoyed every bit of it.

He smacked my ass, and I jumped because it hurt a little bit at first. I got used to it after the fifth smack because it started to turn me on. I loved the way he grabbed my breasts and filled them up in his mouth as he sucked them like they were lollipops. Lying beside him felt so peaceful; I was always afraid for him being out on those streets. I was afraid to fall deeper for him than I already had fallen because I feared something happening to him. Being honest, all of the real niggas end up dead or in jail, and he had already done his jail time. Police were cracking down on our black men, and hell, when they went to prison once, the chance of them going for a really long time became bigger. Those were are all the things that I thought about each time I laid on his warm, bright red body.

Chapter 3: Giving Him My All

Legacy

I guess that's when it happened, the moment we started letting each other in. He started off by letting me know what he did for a living, and he did that by taking me with him on one of his money runs. That's when I saw it, him handing a junkie bag of crack out of the window. I guess the good thing about that was that he didn't take that shit to his parents' home – well, at least not the junkies. After we pulled off, that's when he looked at me and asked, "You think you can handle a nigga like me?" He looked over and waited for my response, and I was a little frightened about him taking his eyes off the road.

"Watch where you're going!" I shouted, afraid for my life because this man wasn't paying any attention at all.

"If you're in love with me that means you wanna deal with a nigga who sells drugs and who drives fast, running from the cops and everything." He pressed his foot down on the gas and started doing eighty on the back streets. I reached for my seatbelt, with my heart skipping a beat, worried that would be my last night breathing. When he noticed that I was scared out of my mind, he slowed down.

"You scared?" he asked, as his hands stayed on the wheel of the car to control it.

"Yes, I'm scared as hell. I've never dated a drug dealer, and I have always been the type to play it safe. I've never fallen in love and always avoided it until you; so, if you really wanna know, Sydney Black, I love you. It scares the shit out of me, but I'm willing to take the risk."

Skrilla leaned over and kissed me once again, and when he looked up, he had swerved over in the next lane a little. He had to do his best to dodge the car that was coming, so he tilted the steering wheel to the right, so we were fully back in our lane. A full week had passed, and he had turned thirty-two, and we spent his birthday together by getting a nice hotel room with a bottle of Cîroc. He didn't like going out to clubs, and he didn't believe in being flashy either because he said that was the dumbest way to get caught by the cops. We bought a radio with us, and I bought along a mixed cd with slow jams on it. I went into the restroom to put on a pair of clear stilettos and a two-piece, red lingerie set, and as he sat on the bed and rolled his blunt, I went and walked out nervously. I turned on the radio and turned the music on while my ass was up in the air, so he wouldn't miss a thing. The music started playing, and the vibe was strong as I moved my body to the beat.

I just wanna show you how much I appreciate you
Wanna show you how much I'm dedicated to you
Wanna show you how much I will forever be true
Wanna show you how much you got your girl feeling good
Wanna show you how much, how much you're understood
Wanna show you how much I value what you say
Not only are you loyal, you're patient with me, babe
Wanna show you how much I really care about your heart
Wanna show you how much I hate being apart
Show you, show you, show you till you're through with me
I wanna keep it how it is, so you can never say how it used to be...

I moved my body the same way Beyoncé did in the video. I put on the best show I possibly could. I wanted him to feel like this show that I was giving him was far better than any strip tease he could get out the strip club or from another woman. Most of all, I wanted him to feel like being there with me, at that moment, was like being in heaven for sure. He pulled my body close to him halfway through the song, and he slid the heels off my feet. His tongue slithered from my neck, down to my stomach, and then, he threw me on the bed to suck on my French

28

manicured toes. I was ready to suck on him as well and mess up my clear lip-gloss that was spread thick on my beautiful, full lips.

"Damn, I can't get enough of you," he whispered in my ear, and that turned me on. I could feel my pussy juices soaking through the bottom of the lingerie that I had on. He slid off the panties and started sucking on my pussy lips while I moaned and held his head to have control.

"Let's do sixty-nine," I suggested as I pulled his head up and waited for him to lay down on his back. I sat my pussy right on his face, pulled down his boxers, and proudly pleased his dick with all the dick sucking strategies I knew. It was almost hard to do because the better I sucked his dick, the more his tongue caressed my pussy in all of the right ways.

That night was everything plus more. After we performed sixty-nine on one another, we made love all night long. We didn't stop until 4 A.M., and we slept the rest of the morning away until it was check out time. We got back to his mother's house, and that was when I was in for another unsettling surprise because his baby's mother had dropped off his daughter, and we had to watch her for the next few days.

"There's Daddy's girl." He kissed his daughter, while he took her out of the car seat, and I stared at her because she was the spitting image of him. His mother didn't like me, so she mugged me as she left for work. She obviously didn't know the full story, and somehow, she had this perception that I was a home wrecker.

"Gosh, she is gorgeous. She is definitely your twin." I took one look at his daughter, and I fell in love with her. Her name was Rihanna, and the only thing she took from her mother, as far as I could tell, was her complexion. Her mother was obviously dark or brown skinned because Rihanna had the most beautiful brown skin complexion. She was only one month old, practically a newborn, and everywhere we went, people thought she was my daughter. Skrilla would always have to correct people when they said we had a beautiful daughter and tell them I was her stepmother. I treated Rihanna as my own, so I didn't understand why he took his time to correct people. I respected her mother fully, but I also knew I was going to play a huge role in this little girl's life as well.

As the weeks went by, it was almost as if we were married. We spent more time together, and when he saw the bond I had with his daughter, I think that made his feelings grow even deeper for me. Everything was good, but that weekend was different. As fast as he came along, things were about to change within the blink of an eye.

"Girl, Skrilla's baby's mother, Tisha, called my house phone while you were gone with him today," my friend, Nyesha, told me as I got dropped off at her house for the rest of the day. I was over her house early that morning, and that's where he picked me up from.

"What did she say?" I asked out of curiosity. I had never spoken to his baby's mother before, and I had only heard negative things about her. I heard that she was a sorry excuse for a mother, and she used her daughter to try and control his life because he left her. I was never the naive type, but I knew these things had some type of truth to it to me, only because I always had his daughter. I guess she thought that if he had his daughter, he would never have time for other women. She was obviously very wrong.

"She said she wants you to call her; her number is on the caller id." Nyesha handed me the phone, and I called her up and then turned on the speaker so that we both could hear her.

"Hello. Did someone call me?" I asked, waiting to see if she knew who she was trying to contact.

"Yes, I was trying to reach Legacy. I wanted to know who you were to Skrilla?" Tisha asked as her voice pretty much cracked. I could feel the tension coming from the other line as I prepared to give my response. This was obviously my chance to find out if she knew who I was and the position I played in his life as well.

"Well, I am Sydney's girlfriend. That's who I am," I told her, waiting to see if she would react like a simple minded girl and curse me out or if she just wanted answers like a woman would.

"His girlfriend? And you know his real name too?" she asked. I could hear the hurt in her voice, not that it really mattered because the only heart I cared about was mine at that point. I guess you can call me selfish, but I had fallen hard as hell, so there wasn't anything this girl could tell me that could help me get back up from that.

"Yes, I am his girlfriend; I know who you are, but you don't need to call me. You need to worry about your daughter because I have her all of the time." I came from a place of honesty, and I wanted her to hurt the way I was hurt by her even calling me.

"First of all, you don't have any reason being around my daughter, and second of all, Sydney and I are still together." She had to redeem herself by any means necessary.

"Well, for you to still be with him, he sure doesn't give you any quality time because he is always with me. As a matter of fact, he just dropped me off. I see the text messages that you send at night, talking about how lonely you are, because I lay beside him every night. So tell me please, when is he ever with you?" I shut everything down with my response. That's when I actually heard her crying through the phone. I didn't give a damn because I was finally happy, and I wasn't going to let her win. The train of thought that I had was that you could have a baby with someone but that still didn't mean that you were meant to be with that person.

"Bitch!" She shouted in my ears right before hanging up the phone. Nyesha stared at me like I was wrong in a way, but fuck all of that because nobody knew how I felt. I was the one lying beside this man all of the time and taking care of his daughter. It wasn't long before he came right back over to my friend's house as if he had already talked to his baby's mother. He jumped out of the car, and he pushed me.

"What the fuck did I do to you?" I asked as a tear came down my face. I was shocked that this man would put his hands on me.

"You told my baby's mama everything, and now she's talking about keeping me away from Rihanna!" he shouted out in anger as he stood there in front of his running car, mugging the hell out of me.

"I gave you everything, all of me, and you lied to me because that bitch told me that you were still together." I cried as I expressed how I felt. I knew the truth because this girl told me, and I wanted him to lie to my face because I was ready to smack the shit out of him.

"Look, we need to stay away from each other." He got into his car and pulled off.

Chapter 4: Break Up to Make Up

Legacy

So many people want to know how do they know if they're truly in love. The only way you really know is when you spend a significant amount of time away from that other person. After week one, I couldn't feel anything good. It was like a weakness in the pit of my stomach, and my heart ached badly. I could feel each beat of my heart, and it was intense yet fast with each moment. When I went outside, I felt a vivid feeling of shame, almost like the world could sense what I was going through. It was August 28th, and everyone was preparing for the season change while I was preparing for the change within my heart. I found myself being excited every time my phone rang, but when I looked at it, I pressed the ignore button whenever I realized it wasn't Sydney calling. I had lost a few pounds because I wasn't happy; therefore, I didn't have an appetite.

After a full month, that's when I saw that call I had hoped for. Surprisingly, after waiting for his call and going over the words that would come out of my mouth when he did call, I didn't answer because I didn't know what to say. After the tenth call and the message saying, "Call me please," I finally gave in to temptation and called him back.

"Hello." I said as I waited for him to say whatever it was that he had to say.

"I've missed you," he said, and it was like the man of my dreams whispering sweet nothings in my ear.

"Missing me is not enough. What have you done to show me that you love me?" I asked; my guard was pretty much back up, and I didn't want to share him with anyone.

"Baby, I got rid of her; I promise. She already knew the whole family thing wouldn't work anyway because I'm in love with you," he said, and I started feeling butterflies again. He had to win me back over though because I wasn't making it easy for him again.

Just like that though, he had me back. We were back to spending time together and being inseparable. As much as he had me, I had him more. Every time I stepped foot out of his car, I knew I was the baddest bitch, his bad bitch. Wearing Jordan's with revealing shorts, a name brand shirt to top the outfit off, and Brazilian weave in my hair, I upgraded from the beauty supply store lip-gloss to Mac lip-gloss. I became his ride or die bitch. I still helped take care of Rihanna, and when she wasn't around, I was riding with him while he made his money, just in case I would ever have to hide some dope inside of my pussy. The love and loyalty was real, and that was all me for real.

Of course, his baby's mother still called, but now, he answered in front of me to let me know that there was nothing going on between them, and he always made it clear that she didn't need to call him unless it was about Rihanna. His baby's mother despised me with a passion, but I didn't have a fuck in the world to give what so ever. On occasion, we would get hotel rooms, just so we could be alone, but this time was different. We went into the hotel office, and this time, I checked in with him. There was a weird guy staring at us, and he picked up his phone and started calling someone. Skrilla looked uneasy when he saw the nigga just sitting there, staring at us. We left the office with our room keys and entered the room, and I could instantly tell Skrilla had something to tell me.

"Hey, baby. You saw that nigga that was in the hotel office?" he asked as he put his bottle of Cîroc and our food on the bed.

"Yes, how could I not see him? He was staring at me, and he started calling someone too." I sat on the hotel bed, not having a care in the world. I always felt safe when I was with Skrilla because he stayed strapped, and he was crazy as hell.

"Well, that's my baby's mama's cousin, and his ass was calling somebody. Damn, he was probably calling her to tell her we are here." He looked out the window to see if he saw her car in the parking lot, but he didn't, so he closed the window back.

"I really don't give a damn. She knows about us, so what is the problem?" I asked him while I sat on the bed and opened his plate of food.

"Yes, she knows about us, but hell, that don't stop nobody from being petty and trying to fight somebody," he said as he came closer to me and slapped me on my hand.

"Why can't I have one of your southwestern egg rolls?" I looked at him and rolled my eyes because he was being stingy.

"Because they're good as hell; if you wanted some southwestern egg rolls, then you should have ordered some instead of those chicken tenders and fries." He took his plate and dipped the egg rolls in some avocado ranch dipping sauce.

I crawled over to him after he finished eating, put my cigarette out in the ashtray, and then I went down on him, giving him the best head a man could ever ask for. He immediately stopped me because he wanted to make love to me, and it felt so fucking good as he put his dick inside of me. I moaned loud as hell and grabbed his back with my acrylic nails as we fucked all night long. I fell asleep and woke up. My hair was fucked up, and it was time for checkout because housekeeping was knocking on the door.

"Wake up, baby; it's time to go." I shoved him, trying to wake him up because I had put the pussy on him so good that he was out for sure. We hurried up and grabbed all the things that we needed to take with us and then left and went downstairs to get into his car. As soon as he turned on the car, an unfamiliar car pulled up and parked right in front of us, blocking our way so that we couldn't get out. I wondered who she was as she got out of the car and went to the driver's side so that he could roll down the window and talk to her. Surely, it was his bitch ass baby's mama. Tisha.

"What the fuck? How are you up here with her, but you were at my house last night?" Tisha asked, standing there, waiting for him to explain.

"Man, I didn't fuck you though. Now, did I?" he asked her like he was surely trying to prove a point to me.

"No, we didn't fuck, but you were still at my house, drinking up my liquor, but then you end up here with her." She placed her hand on her hips and looked at me.

"I didn't need to drink your liquor, but since you offered, hell, why would I refuse? I have my own bottle, but if that's the problem, here goes ten damn dollars for your liquor because my girl and I need to go." He pulled ten dollars out of his pocket and threw it out of the window for her to pick up off the ground. I could see all the hurt on that bitch's face, but I stayed quiet because I knew he had the situation handled. She was lucky that she didn't call me out of my name because I was ready to jump out of the car and fuck her up. She picked up the money, and she got into her car and then drove off. As soon as we got out of the parking lot of the hotel and were passing the Waffle House, I noticed that she had met up with one of her friends at the Waffle House, and she was shouting something. I rolled down the window to see what the bitch had to say that she couldn't say when she was upfront and personal with me.

"That bitch is in the car, and her hair is all fucked up and shit!" she shouted out to her friend.

"Bitch, don't get mad because I'm fucking your baby's daddy; that's why my hair is fucked up. I bet I'm on the way to the hair salon though, bitch!" I was baffled at how this bitch didn't have anything else to say about me, so she brought up my messy hair. I was getting fucked all night in a hotel; hell, whose hair wouldn't be messy? He pulled off because he saw me reach for the door. I was about to get out and whoop that bitch ass, and that's clearly not what he wanted.

"Why the fuck are you pulling off?" I asked as my eyes became low and red, and I mugged him because I was filled with rage.

"Look, I've got bail money, but I don't wanna use that shit. She can't fight, so she ain't gonna do shit but call the police on you."

"Well, you need to tell your non-fighting baby's mama to stay the fuck in her place because these hands don't discriminate period!" I made myself clear as we pulled up in front of the hair salon for me to get my hair done.

He threw five hundred dollars in my lap, as if that was going to help me forget about his dumb ass baby's mama.

"Here, go in there before you're late to your appointment, and then go right over there to get your nails done. I'm picking you up when you finish, so call me." He leaned over and kissed me, but I was still mad at his ass, so I took the money, got out, and then slammed the door.

"You're gonna fuck up my car doing that shit!" He yelled out the window, right before he pulled off, but I knew that nigga wasn't going anywhere, so I didn't give a damn. If he couldn't control his baby's mother, then I had more of a right to act reckless as well.

I went into the hair salon, and I was ready for my sew-in as usual. My hair stylist started washing my hair and allowed me to sit under the dryer so that my hair could dry. After that, she started braiding my hair, and that's when I overheard some bitches talking about my man.

"Yeah, that nigga, Skrilla, has plenty of money. Shit, I can't even fuck with him though because I know his baby's mama," the random bitch said to her friend. Her friend started laughing, and then, she opened her mouth to give her input.

"I heard they weren't together anymore though, so I wonder if he is single right now because what you won't do, I will." She laughed even harder, and I looked dead at both of them bitches, ready to give them a piece of my mind. I had texted him to make sure he was coming back because I was going to wait to get my nails done; I wasn't really in the mood because, with the way things were going, I just felt like I was going to be throwing hands before the day was over with.

"Ummm, Skrilla is my man; his baby's mama knows that much. He is off the market, and I will fuck a bitch up over him real quick." I mugged the bitches and let them know what time it was. I definitely wasn't afraid to fight multiple bitches at the same time because I knew what I was capable of.

"Oh, we see; that's why she has been hurt. Well, at least she can't say that you're ugly because you're pretty as hell. Looks like he upgraded," the bitch who knew his baby mama replied. I damn sure hope she wasn't supposed to be a friend of his baby's mother because if so, that was a foul ass thing to do. That's how bitches were; they were always doing some cutthroat shit and fence riding whenever an opportunity presented itself. As soon as my hair was finished, I noticed his car was parked right in front of the hair salon. Those bitches' mouths dropped to the floor when they realized I wasn't lying.

We were always on the go, and he made it clear that while we were in those streets I didn't have to worry because he had my back and my front. Watching him sell dope to those junkies was uneasy for me, but looking at his swag was such a turn on. He was a low-key big time drug dealer, and he didn't spend his money on fancy shit because he didn't want people knowing how much money he had. He loved to keep it simple, and that's what I liked about him. He was always worried about the Feds, and he didn't want to buy shit that would indicate that he was a dope boy. He was smart as hell, and we knew we could only go up from this moment on.

Chapter 5: From Sydney to Skrilla

Skrilla

I'm Skrilla, but my government name is Sydney. I can be a little bit of a ladies' man, but it wasn't always that way. I started off with both of my parents, shit, but my daddy was a pimp. He was married to my momma, but I remember him being laid off from a factory job that he had, and then he started changing. My mama was loyal as hell to my father; I never saw her with another man. My father was a whole different story because when I got home from school every day, I saw a different girl leave out of our back door before my mother got off work. I guess you can say that's where I get my player ways from.

What women don't understand is that when a nigga cheats, he doesn't carry emotions for the next female. When a woman cheats, hell, she catches all kinds of emotions; the next thing you know, she's ready to leave a nigga and shit for the next one. I was a nerd for a long time; shit, I brought home straight A's and shit. A nigga loved to get homework, and for the most part, I always asked for extra. I was a virgin until the age of eighteen; I hadn't touched a pussy period until I went to college. The first piece of pussy I had was so fucking good that I couldn't get enough of women. I wanted different women, just to feel different kinds of pussy, and that's when I knew I was becoming my father.

My best friend was named Rich, and he sold dope to pay for his tuition. I never knocked what he did; I just didn't want to be involved in that shit. Rich and I used to wild out and fuck all the bitches we could on the campus. Shit, we even made bets on the nerdy bitches who we thought weren;t about that life, and I would win most of the bets we made. I was light skinned, I had a smooth ass face, and all the ladies went for my swag. I wasn't always a drug dealer either, but shit, sometimes the chips fall into that direction when certain obstacles occur in your life. Rich and I were in our sophomore year of college, and this nigga picked me up so we could go and get something to eat from my mom's house. A nigga was tired of eating Ramen Noodles because I didn't have any money like that; shit, I had to take out loans just to pay for my books and tuition.

"What's up, nigga? Let's roll with yo lame ass." Rich pulled up while I was sitting on the bench, trying to get my study game strong.

"Nigga, yo ass is lame. I be pulling more bitches than you," I said, as I put my books into my backpack and went to get into his car.

"Nigga, I can't wait to get to your mom's crib. I know she's got some banging fried chicken, rice, and cabbage for a nigga. Shit, I hope she made some jiffy cornbread, too," Rich said as he got onto the freeway to get there quicker.

"Nigga, slow down. You're driving too fast!" I shouted. This nigga was driving reckless as fuck, and I did have a lot to live for.

I looked into the rearview mirror and saw sirens.

"Damn. I forgot to drop that damn work off!" Rich stated, and then, he started to panic.

"You dumb ass nigga. Damn. Why the fuck did I get in this car with yo ass?" I was mad as fuck, but I told his ass to remain calm because they couldn't search his car unless we allowed them to. When the officer got to the car, this dumb ass nigga started sweating and shit, and the fucking police ended up searching the car any damn way. We both got arrested for two kilos of cocaine, and just like that, my career and life went straight down the drain.

I was nineteen when I went to prison and ended up being in there for a few years. Those were the worst few years of my life. I got out of prison at the age of twenty-one, and the first thing a nigga did was look for a job everywhere. Everyone I went to did a background check, and I always waited for them to call a nigga, but they never did. After five months of looking for a job and being dead broke, I decided to hustle. Hell,

I knew the game a little because of Rich. I started moving little weight, and it turned into big weight. My nickname, Skrilla, came from a regular customer of mine, and somehow, that shit just stuck with a nigga.

Back then, I thought my baby's mama was gonna stay down with a nigga, even though we didn't have any kids together before I went to prison. No matter how many bitches I fucked, she knew her position and she knew I loved her ass. When a nigga went to prison, Tisha had two kids by two different niggas back to back while I was locked up, and that shit hurt like a mothafucka. I then found out that, before I went in, she was already three months pregnant with my baby, but she was under so much stress that she miscarried a week after I got locked up. It fucked a nigga up a little bit, but a nigga had to be strong because I knew I couldn't make it in prison acting like a weak nigga.

Tisha has always been fine as hell; I've always been attracted to dark skinned women. She reminded me of Indie Arie, the same chocolate skin complexion with dreamy, bedroom eyes. She had a fat ass and some nice titties. Her smile was always so big and beautiful, and she was the first girl that I fell in love with. We were together through a lot, and she was always my rider.

When I got locked up, I found out that I got this other chick named Amira pregnant with my son. She carried the baby full term, and when she went into labor at nine months, my son was stillborn. Tisha was hurt as hell, showing up at visitation while I was locked up only to see Amira's name on that list. She dealt with that shit for months, and then, I guess that's when she got tired of my shit and started to fuck around with these clown ass niggas without using protection. I knew she had been faithful for some time, but I guess she wanted me to feel what she was feeling after she found out about Amira.

What she didn't understand was that, after the first child, I was willing to forgive her because it was like she had already gotten even. When the second child came, she was too embarrassed to tell me, but I found out from one of my cousins. The bitch never even admitted it over the phone when I called. She just cried like hell, and I didn't want to hear that shit. When I got out, I got her ass pregnant because it was always gone be my pussy whenever I wanted that shit, and a nigga was horny as a mothafucka. She had the audacity to think I was going to settle down with her, but that shit wasn't going to ever happen. She already had a child before I got with her; she had her first daughter at a young age. When I was in prison, she had two boys by the same nigga, and then, when I got home, I got her ass pregnant with my daughter that first month I was out.

Everything was the same for one full year, until I met Legacy. She was walking down the street, and I stopped because I really wanted to know her name and where she was going. The moment I rolled down that passenger side window and she started talking to me through it, I knew I had to have her. It was love at first sight. I took her to get something to eat and took her to a hotel so that we could spend some time together. I never expected her to go all the way because I could tell that she was a good girl. I'm a real nigga, so I could sense that shit a mile away, but I was happy as hell when we did have sex that night. Not only did this girl have a personality out of this world, but her pussy felt like a bag of diamonds and gold that a broke nigga just found after he'd lost all hope.

I was devastated when she left. Yeah, the condom broke that night, and I knew it did, but it felt so good that I didn't want to stop. Yeah, she was mad as hell, and she left without calling me for a full week. I had many women that came and went, but that week was the first time in my life that I felt so empty. I didn't want to eat or sleep; I kept seeing her face, and that was when I realized that I was madly in love with this girl. She was the reason that no other relationship had worked out in the past, and I knew it. There was only one problem, and that was that I had a hard time trusting any woman because of the things that Trish had done to break my heart. I couldn't stand not seeing her, and I was missing her touch that I had become addicted to, even after only feeling it that one night, so I went looking for her. When I pulled up to where she was at and she got into my car, I knew I wasn't feeling what I felt alone.

I love the fuck out of that girl; she is different, and I never met another girl like her. My baby's mama, Tisha, was something to do for a while until I met Legacy. I know it sounds fucked up, but Tisha is a liar and a manipulator, and she always manipulated me to get whatever she wanted. Tisha didn't know how to love me; she was only infatuated with the thought of locking me down. I needed someone who knew how to love a nigga, and someone I could talk to about anything. I needed someone who would make me feel like having different girls jumping in my bed every night was a dumb ass decision that I didn't need to make.

I need a loyal girl by my side, and I know Legacy is that plus more. She does things with me that no other girl ever did, and she's really down for me. I want to straighten up and be the man she needs me to be; I just don't really know how to, plus I'm afraid. I'm afraid of commitment, and most of all, I'm scared that if I do settle down, I won't be able to give her all the things that she really deserves because of these bullshit ass charges that's on a nigga's record.

Most of all, I'm afraid that I'm going to be just like my father because he never changed. When I look at her, I know she deserves better. She tells me to pray, but I was never taught how. Where was God when I was wrongfully charged for some dope that didn't belong to me? She is the type of girl that won't let me be a drug dealer for long because she's going to want me to get a regular job and shit to take care of her. That's how I know that she is the one, but more than anything, I'm afraid I'm going to fuck up, and she will leave. I ain't never had a bitch that was strong enough to leave me because I'm that nigga, but like I said, she is different from the rest of them.

She gave up so much for me, and she allows our relationship to be about us. She doesn't put anyone in our business; it's just me and her. See, Tisha was, and always has been, another story because, as soon as we went through some shit, her parents, her lonely ass aunt, her fake ass cousin, and her sneaky ass friends were always aware of our business. They were always there with her to tell me that I wasn't shit and to cosign with the shit she was doing. They were always there to aggravate a nigga about not being shit, and they were always pressuring me about doing right by her. I think that's how we grew apart, and I was attracted to Legacy. Legacy is the total opposite of Tisha, and Tisha needs to stop trying to figure out what I see in Legacy because it doesn't even matter.

No matter how many times she pops up at hotels and calls Legacy's phone, my baby, Legacy, ain't going anywhere. Tisha needs to move on with her life and stop trying to ruin the relationship that I have with Legacy. I'm tired of her drama and of her always trying to throw the pussy at me when I go to her house to pick up my daughter. That pussy is ran through, and I don't want that shit. I promised Legacy that I would do right, and even though I still fuck around with random bitches, I try hard as hell for that shit not to get back to her. I stopped fucking with Tisha because that shit is disrespectful and too close to home. Yeah, I'm a dog ass nigga, but there are some things that I refuse to do, even with my reputation.

"Bring that ass over here," I would always tell Legacy, looking at them thick thighs with that fat ass. Her body was sculpted more and more as the months went by, and it was all because a nigga was hitting it right. I should have had more control over the other bitches that I was messing around with because, when they fell in love with a nigga, they got out of line. All of them were side bitches with main chick feelings, and everything I did was starting to catch up with me. I was right in so many ways about Legacy's character, and I knew that she was in love with me. I knew that I was her first love, and I knew she never had a nigga that hit it like I did. It was the way she trembled when she came, it was the way her fingers shook as she held my back, and it was the way her eyes watered while I was inside of her. It was the way she adjusted her schedule so that her life could revolve around mine. I guess the only thing I was wrong about was her not having enough strength to leave a nigga.

Chapter 6: Real Niggas Keep Side Bitches

Legacy

Leaving from that salon, I was amused by the hoes talking about my man. I didn't even bother to tell him though because some things are worth keeping to yourself. We pulled up to his father's house, and while we were still sitting in the car, his baby's mother kept blowing up his phone. He handed me the phone because he was tired of her calling and told me to answer it for him.

"Look, we are really busy right now. We will call you back later." I was happy that he let me do that although she wasn't.

"Whatever, bitch. Put Sydney on the phone!" she shouted like the bothered bitch she was.

"He is right here, and he doesn't want to talk to you. Okay?" I hung up the phone, and the bitch stopped calling, and she started texting his phone. We just ignored her as we went inside his father's house. and he got ready to roll up a blunt. The day had passed us by as we smoked and watched some T.V. together. I couldn't help but feel really sick, and so I ran into the restroom, and I vomited all in the toilet. I thought that maybe it was something I ate, and as he came into the restroom to comfort me, I felt a little better.

There were knocks on the door, and his father had left because he was always on the road with the job he had, so we were the only ones there to answer. Skrilla went to the door, and it was his nigga, Rodney. As soon as I walked out into the living room to see who it was, his nigga became very disrespectful. He looked at me, licked his lips, and said, "Damn, she's sexy as fuck. I need to hit this one, Skrilla."

All of a sudden, Skrilla had punched his ass and pulled him by the collar of his shirt until they were outside in the front yard. He punched him left to right, with a blunt in his mouth, still talking to Rodney. "Nigga, that's my fucking wife; I ain't sharing shit with your disrespectful ass!" He punched him again as he took a hit from his blunt without having to touch it. I ran up to them to get my baby; I didn't want him to go to jail for killing the nigga.

"Baby, please stop!" I shouted as I tried to pull him away from the man. I wrapped my arms around his stomach from the back so he would stop, and he did.

"Now get the fuck out of here, and don't come back before you get merked!" he yelled as he pulled out his gun and waved it all around. I hate to say, but that shit turned me on to the fullest. He was willing to kill over me, and I admired that about him. The last man I had wouldn't bust a damn fly over me, so this was huge for me.

"Baby, we need to leave for a few days and get the fuck away just in case that nigga tries to call the cops or some shit," I said as I continued to comfort him while we headed into the house.

"I don't give a fuck what that bitch nigga tries to do." he said. His whole face turned red because he was mad as hell.

"I know you don't care about that nigga; fuck him. Let's get a room and enjoy ourselves for the weekend, babe." I kissed him and grabbed his dick to let him know what we could do for a whole weekend with no interruptions.

"Okay, baby; just for you." He agreed because why wouldn't he when I knew exactly what to do in order to get my way with him? He went into his room and packed a polo bag with polo socks and underwear; he always told me he couldn't wear clothes that weren't name brand because he would break out really bad. I thought that he had a sense of humor, and he was funny as hell. The good thing about him being picky about what he wore was that he treated his woman the same. He would never allow me to walk around looking like just anything because he always said a woman was a reflection of her man, so it was a must that I matched his fly.

Going into the Marriott, he spent four hundred and ninety dollars on our room, and it was well worth it. Our room had a luscious pillow top mattress, triple sheeting and plush pillows, a 32-inch HDTV, and to top it off, there was a whirlpool Jacuzzi right by the bed.

He promised that he wouldn't take any calls unless they were urgent for the next few days. We fucked like rabbits that Friday and Saturday. My Saturday morning consisted of bagels with cream cheese and a good urban fuck. I used the Jacuzzi to be more appealing because men love when their woman is wet; that shit is a whole different kind of sexy, and his dick stayed hard for me. On Saturday evening, I pulled my hair up, and we ordered some pizza because I didn't want to leave the room.

"Make sure you get chicken and mushrooms with that white sauce on one of those pizzas," he said because he hated pork. At first, he didn't care about me eating it, but it had gotten to the point where he wanted to control me a little, so he wouldn't buy that shit for me either.

"Fine, you've got one lame ass pizza coming right up." I started being sarcastic, and I can honestly say that was one of the things that he did not like about me. I knew because looks told it all.

"Whatever. Come give Daddy's dick some of that good ass pussy before the food gets here." He pulled out his dick and started swinging it around, so I gave him something to make his toes curl. I sucked on the dick like it was going to be the last thing I ever got to suck on before I decided to throw the pussy on him. I turned around when I was finished, and then, I rode him from the back. All he could see was my back, my hair, and my ass bouncing on his dick in a circle. He took out his phone and started to record, which was fine with me because we could watch it later while we ate our pizza together. I must have worn his dick out because he came quickly that time, and he claimed he was tired, so I eased my pussy off of him and then went to take a shower.

I got into the shower and let the warm water hit my body as I rubbed the *Dove* body wash on my body because I never used the soap that the hotel provided. I got out of the shower and reached for the towel to dry my body. I heard Skrilla talking to someone, and I knew it couldn't be the pizza delivery person because they told me thirty minutes and it had only been about seventeen minutes. I turned on the faucet in the sink and cracked the bathroom door, enough to where I could hear him, but he couldn't hear me.

"You know I miss you, baby, but I'm with my peoples right now. I will see you tomorrow sometime." Those words that came from his mouth made my heart drop. I was instantly devastated because I knew there was someone else. A few tears rolled down my face, and then, I pulled myself together so that I could go and confront him like the crazy bitch he was turning me into. With nothing but my towel on, I rushed him while he was lying on that bed to grab his phone and see who the fuck he was talking to. I snatched the phone and ran into the bathroom. Then, I locked the door and sat on the bathroom floor. He followed me, demanding that I give his phone back, but it was way too late. I noticed that the bitch's name was Shannon, and she was still on the phone.

"Yes, this is his fucking wife. Who the fuck are you?" I asked. I wanted to know who she was and how long they had been messing around.

"Look, you need to ask your man who I am," she responded, and then, she hung up the phone.

I opened the bathroom door and shoved the phone in his face.

"So, you're messing with some trifling ass bitches, who apparently know about me?" I asked as I looked at him and expressed that I was hurt. It felt like my spirit was crumbling right there in that hotel room, and he just stood there, staring at me like he knew he had fucked up.

"So, I guess I'm not worth an explanation; furthermore, you couldn't wait until you got away from me to talk to the bitch. I just hope you're using protection because I may just need a trip to the clinic now!" I threw the towel from my body on the floor and headed for my bag. I put on a t-shirt and some jeans with a pair of white Air Forces.

"I'm ready to go home; as a matter of fact, take me to my aunt's house." I picked up the rest of my stuff. He tried to convince me to stay, but he knew he had fucked that all the way up. I left the hotel, and he followed me. We got into his car, and he took me to my aunt's house just like I asked. When we pulled up in the driveway, I opened the glove compartment and grabbed the stack of money that he had there. It was over four thousand dollars.

"I'm keeping this for my troubles." I looked at him as I placed the money in my bra, right under my breast.

"Damn, baby; you're just going to take all the money I have on me? How am I supposed to get gas to make it home?" H looked at me in shock because he didn't think I would react in such a way.

"I guess you can call that bitch, or better yet, suck it up because there is way more where this came from." I walked away and went into my aunt's house. My auntie's name is Calina, and she is my mother's sister, my best friend, and everything good that a girl can ask for. She has always been like my sister and not my aunt.

Walking into the house, she knew something was wrong with me; it's like she could sense it. I burst out crying as soon as the words, "What's wrong," came out of her mouth.

"Auntie, he is cheating on me, and I don't know what to do because I really love him." I went to her and laid my head on her chest as she comforted me and tried to give the best advice that she could possibly give.

"The best thing you can do is ignore that man. Send all of his calls to voicemail and let him know that you won't allow that, baby. Men will only do what they know you will allow," she said, and I trusted her because she knew all about how men operated. She was much older and wiser, so I listened.

I had my own bedroom over her house as well, so that's where I slept as I thought about him every night. My phone wouldn't stop ringing, but I ignored every single call. I remember listening to a Fantasia song called *I'm Doin Me,* and it fit my situation, so I couldn't help but keep it on repeat while I laid in that bed. I was trying to find my worth like she said in the song, and I knew exactly what I did and didn't deserve. A week passed, and my auntie asked me if I was pregnant.

"I don't think so, Auntie? Why would you ask that?" I looked at her as if she was confused at a time like that. Sydney and I weren't even on good terms, so I didn't want to be carrying his child.

"Well, I went to get you a pregnancy test just in case. You eat a lot and sleep a lot. I know you broke up with Sydney, but you are super emotional, baby." She had that look that she usually had when she meant business, so I knew I had to take the test and prove her wrong.

I went into the bathroom and was nervous as hell. I sat on the toilet and placed the pregnancy test right under my private area so that I could urinate directly on it. When I was finished, I waited for a few minutes, and I looked at it to see the results. As soon as the results appeared, my aunt knocked on the door, trying to rush me.

"What does it say?" she asked as I went ahead and opened the bathroom door to tell her what the results said.

"I'm pregnant," I mumbled because I was ashamed. It wasn't so much that she was right; it just wasn't the right time, and I wasn't ready. I wasn't one of those girls who tried to trap a man who had some money. I truly loved Sydney with everything I had in me, and it wasn't even all about that anymore.

"We're having a baby!" she yelled because, clearly, she was happy.

"I don't know what to do, Auntie," I said with disappointment in my voice.

"Baby, you come from a line of strong, single mothers. You will do what you have to do, with or without him." She placed her hands on my shoulders, trying to get me to come to terms with the hand I was dealt.

"Okay, Auntie. Well, obviously, this baby is sleepy. I'm going to get some rest." I hugged her, and then, I went into my room and shut the door.

My eyes watered while I was alone in that room. I heard everything my aunt was saying, but I just didn't feel as strong as I should have. I felt extremely weak as I reminisced about my past, seeing those needles on the ground where I was from and knowing that my mother was abusing drugs and was a drunk that would never change from the looks of it all. Little did I know, I had been dealing with feelings of abandonment for all of those years, just feeling like my mother never wanted me. She used to tell me that I wasn't shit, and I was never going to amount to be anything in life. She said that I would be a failure and a whore. She always tormented me as I grew up in her home, and the minute that I got out was the best feeling in my life. I just wished that I could have left while I was pregnant with London, and I would still have my pride and joy. I had looked for London, and her name wasn't even in the Register Of Deeds anymore. It was obvious that the adoptive parents had changed my baby's name and had probably paid tons of money to cover up their tracks so it would be impossible for me to find her.

The tears started flowing down my gorgeous brown face even harder, smearing the black eye liner that I loved to wear so much. I felt like my life was a roller-coaster ride that I was stuck on for an eternity. I didn't have my father, and that placed the icing on the cake, because I didn't know what real love felt like coming from a man. I was way too young to be capable of telling the difference from lust and true love. The only thing I knew was that my heart ached for Sydney, and I never knew

I could hurt so bad while carrying strong feelings for someone. I buried myself into my pillow and cried until my eyes were puffy.

I turned my phone on silent because I didn't feel like talking to anyone. I was so confused and didn't know what to do. I had gone from a man that was respectful, but didn't know how to be my protector, to a man who had groupies and couldn't protect my heart. My aunt was right, and I had to learn to stand on my own two feet. I had felt sorry for myself for far too long, and I needed to make the change in my life that I wanted to see. I had drowned myself in my confusion, and things couldn't get worse than they possibly were. All of the feelings I never thought I could feel, I felt them all, and I really needed someone to come to my rescue and take the endless pain away.

Chapter 7: A Complicated Love

Legacy

I laid in my bed and fell asleep to the sound of the rain. It was late when I heard knocks on my window. As I wiped my eyes to see who it was, I looked up, and it was Skrilla standing there, looking at me through the window. The window's blind was halfway open because I loved looking at the rain until I fell asleep. I got out of my bed, with nothing on but a tank top and some panties, and went to see what he could possibly want at that time of the morning.

"Hey, what's up?" I said, wiping my eyes and yawning as he stood in the doorway.

"You gonna let me in? I'm getting wet out here." He stood there, getting hit by the rain, and then, I finally let him in.

He followed me to my bedroom, and I shut the door behind him, and then I sat on my bed. He got on his knees and began kissing my thighs, and he stared at me and started crying.

"I'm sorry about those hoes. I love you, and it took me some time to realize it, but you're the best thing in my life. You're loyal, and you love me for who I am. Those other bitches ain't gonna be there if I lose everything, but I know you will."

"That's all I wanted you to know; I don't give a damn about your money. Hell, it's good to have someone who is capable of doing things for me whenever they can, but at the end of the day, all I really want is you." I grabbed his face and kissed him.

"You don't have to worry about no hoes, I promise, and I'm not going anywhere." He kissed me back, and then, he took my clothes off and got into the bed with me. We made love while listening to the sound of the rain hitting my window, and it was beyond beautiful. As we laid there, I couldn't help but tell him the news because I didn't want to keep any secrets from him.

"Baby, there is something important that I have to tell you," I softly whispered in his ear, while I tried to find the words.

"What's wrong; you haven't been cheating on me have you?" He looked at me. There was nothing but my T.V. on, but I could clearly see his gorgeous eyes.

"I took a pregnancy test; my auntie forced me to take one, and it was positive," I said, waiting for him to respond. I thought he was going to be upset because, with all of the drama going on with his other baby's mother, I didn't think he wanted any children any time soon.

"So, you're having my baby?" he asked with a smile on his face.

"Yes, I am... Hopefully, a little baby boy that looks like you, or a girl that looks just like me." I replied as he hugged me tighter. We fell asleep in one another arms that night, and we were happy once again. I finally had my family that I wanted, and although it was coming sooner than I thought it would, I felt complete.

A few months had passed, and I was about to go to my first doctor's appointment to check on my baby. My stomach was still small, so I couldn't be that far along. I was still staying at my aunt's house, and I had gotten a job working at Captain Ds because my aunt taught me that no matter how much money a nigga had, never let them feel like you were depending on them. I was making minimum wage, and I hated it; hell, I was too pretty to smell like fish because of where I clocked in at. There were different guys at my job who had crushes on me, but my heart and body both belonged to Sydney. That morning that we went to the doctor we were super excited about checking on the baby. Although he couldn't come in with me because he had money runs to make, I was okay with that.

"Hello. I am Doctor Allen Smith, and I will be taking care of you today," the doctor said as I sat in the room, waiting for him. I went to a private doctor's office, so I didn't have to wait that long to be seen.

"Okay, I'm so excited to check on my baby. I could barely sleep last night," I replied as I waited for him to do whatever he was about to do.

"I'm about to check your cervix to see how far along you are, and then, we are going to run some tests and check on the baby's heartbeat today," the doctor said as he got the nurse to come into the room to supervise the procedure. I felt the discomfort as the doctor checked my cervix after he placed on some gloves. Then, he took some long Q-tips and swabbed the walls of my vagina and placed them into a cup. Then, when he was done with all of that, he put some lubricant jelly on my belly, which was cold at first, to check the baby's heartbeat. I could see by the expression on the doctor's face that something was terribly wrong, but he didn't say anything. It was about fifteen minutes of waiting to see what they had to say before they came back into my room.

"I have some bad news." Doctor Allen Smith looked at me, and I knew something was terribly wrong.

"What is it? Am I doing too much at work? Is it my health?" I asked, wanting to know what was so bad.

"I'm sorry, Ms. Hayes, but you are three months along, and the baby has no heartbeat." I could tell that he dreaded telling me that type of news. I cried like a baby, right there on the bed, and the doctor left the room and allowed me to have some time alone. I was told that I had already started miscarrying, and my baby would be stillborn, and I was beyond devastated. Walking outside of that clinic to see Skrilla, sitting in that car, with a smile on my face, just made my heart beat faster. I didn't want to tell him that our baby had died because I didn't want him blaming me. He had told me not to take that job at Captain D's, and I didn't listen because I thought he was trying to control my every move. I stepped into the car and sat down as he asked how the appointment went.

"How's my son doing? Because I know it's going to be a boy," he asked with excitement in his eyes.

"I lost the baby." I cried out as I closed my eyes and hoped I was having a nightmare.

"How did you lose the baby?" he asked with confusion.

"The baby is dead, and the doctor told me I will probably miscarry at home." I looked at him, and I noticed a tear coming down his face as he drove off. He was numb, and he didn't say anything else for the remainder of the drive. He dropped me off at my aunt's house, and I ended up quitting my job at Captain D's because I felt like if I had never taken that job so quickly, all of this would have never happened.

I was falling into a world of depression; I didn't want to eat nor come out of my room. I was on bedrest, and I had to wait to miscarry my baby. Skrilla had started drinking more than he usually would, and I was afraid for him because he always drove around a lot. A week after that doctor's appointment, I started having heavy cramps, and I got up to use the bathroom. I fell to the floor because I was in so much pain that I couldn't walk.

"Ahhh, oh my God... Uggghhh... Auntie!" I screamed out in agonizing pain as my aunt got up from her sleep, and she helped me pull my underwear down. The fetus, which would have been my pride and joy, slithered from the walls of my vagina, off my legs, and onto the carpet while I laid on the hallway floor. My auntie called the paramedics as I laid there waiting for them to get there. They arrived immediately, and they asked my aunt if she had a Ziploc bag to put the baby in, and so she got one for them. I cried, and my aunt cried with me as she tried to help me up, and she went and got a washcloth to help clean me up with. I texted Skrilla to let him know what happened, and he got there while the paramedics were still there because they wanted to make sure that I was alright.

"Ma'am, you need to go to the emergency room because you will need to have surgery done to get the amniotic sac out of you," one of the paramedics explained, while checking my blood pressure.

"Okay, my fiancé will take me." I looked at Sydney, and I could see the hurt in his eyes. The look on his face when he saw the fetus in the Ziploc bag was something unbearable. I could tell that was one of the worst days of his life, and it was one of mine as well.

Chapter 8: They Want What's Mine

Legacy

Leaving from that hospital, I was feeling very weak. However, I was happy that he was right there by my side.

"Baby, you want something from the store?" he asked as he parked at a gas station to get some gas, not too far from the hospital.

"No, I'm alright… The only thing I want is sleep." I turned at him, and let him know I didn't need anything and that I was extremely tired.

"Okay, but I'm taking you to get something to eat because, baby, you are on antibiotics and pain medications, so you need to eat something with those pills." He kissed me as he got out of the car and went into the gas station to pay for gas. As soon as he came out and started pumping, some unfamiliar car pulled up beside us and some girls got out. One of them walked over to Skrilla, and my window was cracked, so I could hear everything.

"Look, y'all need to go on with that bullshit now. I'm with my girl, and she doesn't feel good," Skrilla said. The body expression he had showed that he was ready to fight them himself if he had to, but I just didn't know what it was all about.

"Look, you thought you were gone get rid of me for this bitch, Skrilla?" She looked at him with her hands on her hips, and I could tell she was some ratchet ass hood rat he used to fuck with.

"Look, I don't want to have to hurt your fucking feelings, but you weren't shit but a late night fuck, and this is my woman. Now, you and your friends need to get the fuck out of here with that bullshit before I slap the fuck out of all of y'all." I smiled, even though I was hurting, because I knew my man had that shit taken care of once again. I was just so mad that I had just gotten out of the hospital and was doped up on pain medicines because I would have beat the fuck out of all them bitches myself, right at that damn gas station.

Those hoes got into their car and pulled off so fast that I thought they were going to wreck on the way out of the gas station. He finished pumping his gas and then got back into the car.

"I'm sorry about that bullshit, baby. I told you that I cut people off for you, so those busted ass hoes are mad as hell because I'm a one-woman man now." He looked at me as he cranked up the car and pulled out to take me home.

"It's okay, baby. They're lucky that I'm not feeling well because I would have fucked them up myself." I barely smiled as I told him how I would have reacted if I would have felt better and wasn't high off of medication.

More than anything, He was happy that I wasn't upset with him. One month had passed, and it was getting cold. It was the middle of November, and it felt like it was going to snow already. Before you knew it, Thanksgiving had come and gone, but he wasn't here with me like he was supposed to be for that whole day. He made up some excuse about not wanting to eat the pork my family had prepared, so he picked me up later on that day and took me to his father's house so I could eat Thanksgiving dinner with them. Something about that was pretty fishy to me, but I didn't question it at all because he did show some type of efforts to be with me.

December had come, and Christmas morning was no different because he claimed he had to spend time with his daughter, and although I was upset that he was at his baby's mother's house, I still didn't complain about that either.

I started wondering, just like any other woman would. I was being very loyal to this man and hadn't cheated on him since we had been together, so I deserved to know if he had been up to his old games. His phone rang all the time, and I knew that it wasn't always a crack head on that other line. One night, he had fallen asleep while we were at his mother's house, so I picked up his phone because it was beeping. I couldn't tell whose number was whose because the names were all abbreviated, but I could go through his text messages.

Shay- Baby, I need you. Please answer...

Shay- I'm drunk, and I want to see you...

Shay- I'm on my way to your mother's house. You weren't at your dad's.

I stared at him while he was sleeping with a frown on my face. I thought about all of the shit I could do to him, while he was asleep, to make his ass pay. Surely, I was in love, but hell, I've never been a dumb ass bitch. I knew for sure that these hoes weren't doing the most for no reason. He was still fucking around with them, and I was sick of his shit. It was like having a dog that you tried to train constantly, over and over, yet no matter how hard you tried, they still shitted all over your freshly cleaned carpet.

There was a horn blown outside of his mother's house, and he woke right up out of his precious, deep sleep. "Who the hell is that?" he asked, while getting up and attempting to throw some clothes on.

"Something tells me that it's the drunk bitch named Shay who keeps on texting you and shit." I smiled because I knew he hated situations like that. He ran to the door, and I knew there was going to be conflict, but that was his fucking problem. I was tired of trying to fight over him because that shit was played out.

"Get your drunk ass friend out my yard, and get the fuck out of here!" he shouted, and as I looked out of the window, I saw the bitch laying in his front yard, crying and throwing up.

"I love you, Sydney!" she said as she vomited all over herself.

"Man, you need to get out of the car and get your friend because my lady is in the house with me; she knows I've got a woman." he said, right before he came back into the house, slammed and locked the door.

He came in the room, trying to explain, but I was about to give them hoes what they wanted and let them have his hoe ass.

"I need to go home." I unwrapped my hair and put it in a ponytail because I was ready to fuck him up.

"Look, I know you're probably mad, but fuck those bitches because I'm keeping it real with you. You already know what the fuck I used to do, and I never had to tell you any of that shit!" he yelled as he pushed me on the bed because he didn't want me to go anywhere.

I started crying because I was tired of going out of the way for him and dealing with these hoes who just didn't understand that no means hell no.

"Well, this shit needs to stop because I don't know how much more I can take." I sat up and held my hands over my face while the tears kept coming. He wiped my tears, pulled out three stacks of money, and then threw it all over the bed. He took my clothes off and whispered in my ear.

"Baby, I wanna fuck you on this money tonight." He started kissing my neck and then sucked on my breast. How could I resist when his dick was hard, and I wanted every bit of those nine inches deep inside of me? I also loved the thickness of his dick because he could always fill me up in the best way. Every time we fucked, I started understanding why all of these hoes were infatuated with him. Not only was he a real nigga, but he had plenty of money, a big dick, and his pipe game was out of this world.

"Yes, baby. Give me that good ass dick!" I moaned and screamed as I felt his good ass dick penetrating every inch of my slippery, yet tight, walls.

"Turn around and let me see that pretty face." He had me bent over, and he always loved to look at my face while he was hitting it from the back. As soon as I looked at him, I started moaning and calling his name. It felt like his dick got even harder, and I loved that shit. The dick was so excellent, so of course, it put my ass to sleep and made me not even aggravate him because I was no longer worried about other bitches. I was going to play my position.

As the months passed, we were fine, and although he was a ladies man, he hustled hard to make sure that I was straight and so was his daughter. My bond with his daughter grew strong as she got older, and there was nobody who couldn't tell me I wasn't her stepmother to be. I was the boss bitch in charge, and I felt my power within my position. That is, until one day, I was hanging out with my friends, and we went to the mall. What I saw that day in the spring nearly broke my heart. I saw a girl walking with a baby who looked like him, so I walked up to the girl and attempted to get some information.

"Hello. How are you doing?" I asked while putting on a fake smile, just to get my way.

"I'm doing well," she replied in a standoffish manner.

"I just came over because your baby looks just like my cousin," I said, standing in a welcoming manner and waiting for her to tell me something I wanted to know. Although I wanted to find the truth out, I dreaded her saying my boyfriend's name.

"What's your cousin name?" she asked.

"His name is Sydney." I replied. I knew that if this was his baby, she could possibly know him by his government, and not his street, name.

"Her father is named Sydney," she replied.

"Well, she is completely beautiful," I said, smiling at her and her daughter before I walked away. I didn't even bother to get her name because it didn't even matter. The baby had to be around five months old, and here I am, thinking that he was a hoe, but he used protection whenever he did step out on me. I was so wrong on so many levels, and all I wanted to do was confront him.

My friends and I left, and we rushed over to his father's house. As we pulled over in front of the driveway, there was an unfamiliar car there. I got out, went to the door, and knocked. When he opened the door, I saw that his cousin was over there, but I didn't give a damn.

"I just want you to know that I saw your other baby's mother at the mall today, and your daughter looks just like you." I frowned, waiting for him to lie so I could flip out of my mind.

"I don't know what you're talking about. Are you okay?" He placed his hand on my forehead as if I was running a fever or something.

"I'm perfectly fine, but you're not about to be." I smacked his hand off of my face and pushed him away from me.

"Man, do you know how many females done tried to pin babies on me before?" he looked at me and asked.

"I don't give a damn because this is the last time; they can have you." I walked out of the house and left with my friends. It was either that he was lying to me or that he had other kids out here that he was denying and not taking care of. Neither of those scenarios were looking good at all. Every woman has their breaking point, and they get tired of being faithful to a man who wasn't giving his all back to them. I was about to do whatever I wanted and sleep with whoever I wanted to.

I was about to be nineteen years old, and although I had done a lot in my life, there was so much more for me to see and do. I wasn't raised to be a fool, and I definitely wasn't born yesterday, so he couldn't just keep running game on me and think that I wasn't going anywhere. I had to make a huge statement somehow and get his attention. I am not afraid to stand-alone and have fun alone, so I planned a trip to Atlanta all by myself. After all, you don't take sand to the beach. Right?

I booked a hotel in downtown Atlanta, and I packed my bags, picked up my rental car, and headed to the A.

Chapter 9: Finally Doing Me

Legacy

I hit the highway with my phone on silent and my music up loud. I was looking fly, had my hair done with pin up curls, and had some fire red lipstick on. My black eye liner was on with some red eye shadow. I had a tight red and black maxi dress on, and my Red Bottoms were sitting on the passenger seat because I hated wearing heels while I was driving; it didn't matter the distance. My nails were perfect; they were dark blue with different designs on every finger, and I had them done right before hitting the road. It was time to do something different and step back into being my wild and free self for a while.

I stopped at a gas station to get something to drink and some gas as soon as I arrived in Georgia. I reached for my Red Bottom heels as soon as I parked my car and put them on my feet. The gas station was packed full of people, and stepping out, I knew I was the shit.

"Damn, shawty. Where's your man at?" I heard the random niggas going crazy over me. I wasn't sure if it was my pretty face, my outfit that hugged my body tightly, or the curves that filled the dress I wore with perfection.

"Sorry, I have a man," I responded. I didn't want any of them. I only wanted to get my feet wet a little and see if I still had it. The guy that I met and decided to sleep with had to be perfect; well, not perfect but he had to at least make me feel like I wasn't downgrading for a piece of dick. I got my gummy worms and my peach soda, and then, I pumped my thirty dollars' worth of gas. That's why I loved driving compact cars; the gas was so affordable. When I finished, I got back into my car, took my shoes off, and then proceeded to make it to downtown Atlanta.

I turned my music up loud and started singing the lyrics to the song that was playing from my CD. I stuffed the gummy worms into my mouth using my left hand, while I controlled the steering wheel with my right hand.

I made it to the hotel and checked in. Going to the room, I realized I had the most beautiful view, looking over everything in downtown Atlanta. I unpacked some of my things because I was going to be in Georgia for as long as I needed to be. I had five thousand dollars that I had been stashing from Skrilla, so I was going to treat myself as much as possible. I made a trip to Lenox Mall and got myself some fly outfits to wear to the club, and then, I hit my girl, Tashawna, up to see what she was doing for the day. Tashawna had an overprotective boyfriend who always smothered her, so it was a breath of fresh air to get out every once in a while.

"What's up Tashawna; what are you doing for the day?" I asked while I drove, trying to make it back to the hotel. I had so many bags, and more than anything, I loved Victoria's Secret, so I stocked up on all the sexy lingerie and smell good lotions.

"Girl, I'm ready to get out of this house," she said, sounding extremely bored.

"Well... I am in town for a while, so we can meet up today if you'd like," I said, trying to make it through the terrible traffic to get back to the hotel room.

"Okay. I will catch the bus. Just pick me up from the bus station in Decatur," she suggested.

"Okay, I will be there within the next hour." I hung up the phone and was able to get to the hotel ten minutes later. I dropped off my things and then headed back out because it was going to take me a little while to get through the terrible traffic to get to Decatur. Although I had stayed in Atlanta before, I was still learning my way around, so I used my GPS to get there. I turned up my music to help me not get frustrated with the traffic; it was always bad. Hell, people acted as if they couldn't drive in North Carolina; those same people would never make it behind the wheel in Atlanta.

I finally pulled up to the bus station, and Tashawna was there, waiting on me in the front. I stepped out to give my girl a hug and glanced a little to the left, and that's when I saw him. He was standing there, holding a backpack with his work uniform on. I was hoping he wouldn't see me, because the whole vibe would have been a little too uncomfortable, but as soon as I turned around and was about to get into my car, that is when I heard his voice.

"Legacy, I know that's you." He called out my name, and while Tae got into the car, I slowly turned around so that I could see what he was about to say. I hadn't spoken to this man in over a year, the exact same amount of time that I had been dating Skrilla. I told Tae that I was coming and walked over to greet him.

"Hey, stranger; how are you doing?" he asked me as I took a cigarette out of my purse and lit it up.

"I have been doing pretty good; how about you?" I asked. Although we had broken up and gone our separate ways, I still wanted the best for him, and I hoped he was happy.

"I have been doing okay, I guess, but it's a surprise to bump into you in Atlanta. You still stay in North Carolina; don't ya?" he asked as he came a little closer.

"Yes, I still stay in North Carolina; I'm just visiting for a little while." I threw the remainder of my cigarette on the ground and looked back because I still had the car running.

"If I call you, will you answer?" he asked, and he looked nervous, almost as if I were to say no, it would completely break his heart.

"Yes, I will answer. Just call me later on tonight; I was going out, but I will probably just hang out with my friend."

That smile that he had on his face though; it was almost as if I could sense that it had been a while since he had smiled like that.

I gave him a hug, and then, I got into my car and pulled off as he watched me drive away. I turned my radio on, and my song was on, so I started feeling the music because it fit my situation.

> I used to think that I wasn't fine enough
> And I used to think that I wasn't wild enough
> But I won't waste my time trying to figure out
> Why you're playing games, what's this all about
> And I can't believe your hurting me
> I met your girl what a difference
> What you see in her
> You ain't seen in me
> But I guess it all was just make-believe
> Ohhh love never knew what I was missing
> But I knew once we start kissing I found, found you...

We got back to the hotel and went inside my room. The thing I liked about Tashawna was that she was down for whatever. It didn't even matter if she stayed overnight. Hell, it was Friday, and her daughter was gone with her mother for the weekend. I had taught her well. Stay away from a nigga for a little while; you giving him space and not smothering him will make that nigga get his mind right quickly.

"Girl, you didn't bring any extra clothes?" I asked her because I wanted to go out to the strip club that night.

"Nope, I was going to find something to wear. Maybe go shopping," she added. She was my girl, and I was always one step ahead, so I knew exactly what to do because I sure as hell wasn't going back to Lenox Mall.

"Girl, I've got you. We don't have to go out to Lenox because I've already been," I told her as I pulled out the bags of stuff I had bought. Of course, I had first dibs on the stuff I bought, but I gave her a few outfits to pick from. I wear a size ten, and she wore a size nine. We were about the same size; the only difference was that I had a fatter ass and some thicker thighs. The skintight dresses that I bought were going to be perfect for us. We also both wore a size eight in shoes, and we were both the same height.

Nightfall had approached; and I took a shower and put on my skintight white and black dress. Tashawna wore a blue and black one. We both wore Red Bottoms to match our dresses and carried Michael Kors' purses. We left as soon as we knew we were beyond cute and ended up at Onyx Strip Club. As soon as we entered, it was beyond packed. The music was so loud in my ears, as they played the hit song, *Commas,* by Future.

"It'll be twenty dollars to get it," the lady at the front desk told us as I went into my purse to pay our way in.

"I've got you, Tae. Just buy your drinks and get some lap dances tonight. You probably need them," I informed her as we walked to the area where the bar was. There was a two-drink minimum, and the shots of liquor were ten dollars per shot. I knew I was going to get wasted because Tae didn't drink like that, and she had her license as well. After chugging down the shots, we made our way to the stage to see the female dancers. We both were strictly dickly, but we loved, and supported the dancers because they were out here making a living just like everyone else. When this stripper named Moet hit the stage, I knew she deserved all of my tips because, not only could she dance her ass off, she knew how to do all type of tricks on the pole. By the time we left, I had spent over three hundred dollars in that club. I was so faded that I had to take off my Red Bottoms just so I wouldn't fall on my face.

"Here you go, Tae. You drive." I handed her the keys to the car. I wasn't trying to wreck the car, and I was worrying about our safety and the expenses I would pay for a wrecked rental car.

We got into the car, and I was hungry as hell. Although the club had food, I never ate the food at strip clubs.

"I'm hungry. Let's go to Waffle House or something," I stuttered as we rolled down the street, attempting to get to our destination.

We finally got to the Waffle House, and I was hungry as hell. I ordered my favorite, which is the all-star breakfast - waffles, grits with cheese, scrambled eggs, toast, and bacon.

We took the food to the hotel because I was too wasted to sit and eat under all of those lights. As soon as we entered the room, that's when Tae reminded me of something.

"Wasn't your ex-boyfriend supposed to be calling you?" she asked as she indulged in her breakfast. It was 2 A.M., but it was good to her as well, I could tell.

"Oh, shit. I haven't even checked my phone." I took my phone out of my purse, and I had over ten missed calls from him. I felt awful because I didn't want him to think that I was ignoring him.

Instead of calling him, because that would have been rude since I had company, I just texted him and told him that I'd call him the next day after I dropped Tae back off at home. I could only imagine how pissed her boyfriend was because he was calling so much that she just silenced her phone. I ate so much that I instantly felt stuffed, and then, the next thing you know, I woke up around 10 A.M.

"Oh, God. How in the hell did I fall asleep without even realizing it?" I looked around, and I started shaking Tae to wake her up. We had the empty plates of our food on the nightstand and didn't even bother to throw anything away in the trash.

"Come on, girl, before your man ends up in jail, and we both end up on First 48," I told Tae, as she hurried up and changed her clothes. She wouldn't dare walk into her apartment with that outfit on, but she sure was going to take it with her. She wore it so it belonged to her now. It seemed as if we rushed in traffic; I was glad that I didn't get a ticket or get into a wreck. I dropped her off and waited five minutes to make sure she was okay. She called me and told me that she was, and if she hadn't, I knew to go ahead and call the police. As soon as I pulled out of her apartment complex, I called Vonne, and he answered, sounding all excited to hear my voice.

"Hey, I'm sorry I didn't answer, but I went out with my girl last night." I was starving while talking to him, so I decided to stop by a wing stand and get something to eat.

"That's okay, but what are you doing?" he asked, and I knew where it was going. He wanted to see me, and he was going to ask if that was possible.

"Going to get something to eat; I'm beyond starved." I answered as I pulled up at the wing stop.

"What are you getting to eat?" he asked, and then, he paused waiting for me to tell him. Nothing had changed; he was still the same person. Back then, he wanted to know everything about me, and I never thought he was a stalker like I would have if he were another man. He wanted to know what I was eating, what music I listened to, what kind of soap I showered with, and the name of the fragrances that I wore. Most of all, he always wanted to hear about my hopes and dreams, and he always hoped he was a part of my dreams as well.

"I'm going to get some hot wings and fries." I answered as I got out of the car and went to the window to order my food.

"Hot wings, fries, and some blue cheese on the side with a fruit punch to drink, please." I ordered as I heard him breathe on the other line, just listening to my voice.

"You need to bring me some of that. I'm hungry too." he said, and I knew that was his way of trying to get my company. I sure didn't see anything wrong with it either.

"Are you serious?" I asked, just to make sure.

"As a heart attack," he answered, so I went on to order what I knew he wanted.

"I need another one of those but with ranch instead of blue cheese and extra carrot sticks on the side." I ordered and then waited for the food to be ready. The smell coming from that wing place made my mouth water, and that's what I loved about Atlanta. There were always a variety of food spots that you definitely couldn't find in North Carolina. When the food was ready, I paid fourteen dollars and seventy-six cents and then headed to the address he gave me. He wanted to stay on the phone because he said he was all that I needed, and although that part annoyed me, I just went along with it. Crazy as it was, I didn't have any plans of leading him on, but I didn't tell him anything about Skrilla. I definitely didn't want to break his heart, and I knew that would most likely do it.

Chapter 10: A Real Man Like Me

Vonne

I was born and raised in Decatur, Georgia, and my name is Vonne Moore. I was raised by both of my parents until the age of thirteen, and then, my father died from a stroke. My mother then had to raise me all by herself, and I appreciate what she has done for me. Before my father passed away, my mother didn't have to work, and when he passed, she had to maintain two jobs, a car payment, and mortgage all on her own. I graduated from high school and went to college as well. I graduated with a degree in business. My dreams were to have a wife one day, treat her with respect, and be faithful to her. I learned from my father because they had been together for twenty years, and he always looked at her the same. There were times when she would be sitting on the sofa reading, and he would turn on some old school music and ask her to dance with him. Their lives were beautiful, and I'm glad he installed all of the things that he did in me because I didn't turn out to be a thug, whose life isn't going anywhere. I really don't surround myself around certain people because I've never been the stupid type. I know that you can get caught up, and you are your circle.

After I got my degree, I understood that a business wasn't going to be given to me, so I decided to work from ground up. I didn't want to stay with my mother forever, so I started looking for a job. Charlotte, North Carolina was appealing to me because of an opening at Merita Bakery's Warehouse. The job paid seventeen dollars an hour, so I decided to take a leap of faith and apply. It had only been a week after I applied, and they were calling me, asking to interview. I packed my bags and decided to go ahead and move down there; I had a good feeling that the job was mine, so there was no need to waste any time.

Getting there, I was kind of nervous. I had never been to North Carolina before, but I knew God had me one hundred percent. I stayed in a cheap motel and went to the interview, which I bagged, just like I knew I would. Staying in that motel for a full month was extremely hard, seeing those drug addicts and having to watch my step each time I walked outside of the hotel because of the needles that were lying on the ground. I couldn't take much of that, so I knew I had to find a roommate quickly. Yes, I could have gotten my own apartment, but it would have taken much longer, and I needed to get out of that hellhole fast.

I got the Sunday's classified paper, and there was one that stood out. A guy named Joey was looking for a roommate. He already had one roommate, which meant we could split the rent three ways, and I could save more money quicker and be in my own place in no time.

"Hello, Joey. I'm Vonne, and I just moved to Georgia; I'm calling about the roommate ad you placed in the newspaper," was how it all begun. Initially, we spoke for about twenty minutes, and we had a lot of things in common. Just like everyone else, I had flaws and mine were that I like to occasionally smoke and drink, and so did he. Moving in with him was perfect because he didn't stay too far from my job.

One day, we were walking to the store together to get some cigars and some snacks, and that's when it happened. I bumped into the most beautiful girl in the world. Her name was Legacy, and it was love at first sight for me. She was beautiful. She was a little rough around the edges, because of the horrible events that occurred in her life, but I loved that about her. She reminded me of my mother because my mother had been through things that were similar to her situation. I knew all of her hopes and dreams, and I wanted to be her provider and make her dreams come true.

That day I met her was the best day of my life. I just knew I was going to take her to Georgia to meet my mother, so my mother could get a chance to see in this girl what I saw in her. I had been working extra hard ever since I fell in love with her, saving up as much money as I could. Things took a turn for the worse when my roommate found his dream house, and we moved from the apartment that we stayed in. I told my roommate shortly after we moved that I had found an apartment, and I was going to move within the next few weeks. I had already paid a deposit and everything, and Legacy was going through some things. I knew this would surely help us regain custody of her daughter, London.

I had found a lawyer and planned on approaching him as soon as we moved and were situated. I spent fifteen hundred dollars on an engagement ring, and the next week, I took two days off of work because I knew she was going to be off for those two days as well. The same day that the fight broke out with my roommate was the same day I was going to take her to our new apartment that was already paid for.

My roommate was tripping, and I knew it was behind me leaving. That house that he forced us to move into was fifteen hundred dollars a month, and I made the most income in the house, so I knew he couldn't afford it. I placed Legacy first and my roommates on the backburner because I loved her more than anything, for sure.

When she walked out of my life that day, I attempted to reach out to her, but I was unsuccessful. After a few weeks of not speaking to her, I finally got my money back from the apartment; I put my two-week notice in with Merita Bakery, and I moved back to Georgia to stay with my mom. I took that money and helped my mother with her bills, but there wasn't a day that went by that I didn't speak of Legacy to my mother and the rest of my family. I even had an ex-girlfriend who tried to re-enter my life, but I couldn't do that because I was patiently waiting for Legacy to come back.

I got the job that I told her I was going to get at KFC. I worked myself up from shift leader to assistant manager and from assistant manager to general manager. I just couldn't wait for that phone call from her because, if I were to ever get her back, I would do everything in my power to keep her happy and make sure she never left again.

I can't seem to replace this girl because she is irreplaceable. Her eyes, the way she smiles, and everything about her is remarkable. She is beautiful, but sometimes, I can sense her insecurities. I can tell she only wants a man who can give her the best things in life; and I know I deserve her. She doesn't deserve a nigga who is risking his life selling drugs, trying to make fast money because she doesn't deserve to be hurt because her man ends up dead or in jail. I will work two jobs if I have to in order to care for her. I will put my life on the line for her, but she doesn't see that because I wouldn't sit there and fight a dumb ass battle with my roommate - only because I had bigger and better plans for her anyway. At night, I can't sleep without her by my side; I can't eat because she is no longer beside me, picking over her food, taking forever to stuff her face. I love the way she chews her food as she eats and the way she loved to watch movies while she is lying in the bed.

I'm far from stupid, and I know there may be someone else. A girl as beautiful as she is doesn't dump a guy and sits there, waiting for him to meet her standards before she takes him back. I am a God fearing man, and I've prayed on the situation every night before I go to bed, so that day that I ran into her here in Atlanta, I knew that was God, answering my prayers.

Chapter 11: A Few Days with Vonne

Legacy

I took that trip to Decatur to take Vonne the food he had requested. Pulling up in front of his house, I was nervous as hell. Walking up to the door, getting ready to ring the doorbell, I was shitting bricks. Right before I rang the doorbell, the door was opened, and there he was, standing there, smiling at me.

"Well, are you going to stand there and stare at me, or are you going to let me in before this food gets cold?" I stood there, holding the bag with the food and the cup holder with the drinks in the other hand.

"I'm sorry, but you look so beautiful," he explained as he opened the door and took the drink tray out of my hand.

I walked into the house, looking around because it looked like an older person decorated, instead of someone vibrant and young.

"Excuse the house; I'm staying with my mother. I have to take care of her because she is really sick." He looked into my eyes as he led the way to his bedroom.

"I'm so sorry to hear about your mother; it must be really hard on you right now." I looked into his eyes as I placed the food down on the nightstand in his bedroom. I could look into his eyes and tell that he wasn't really happy. I could see that he was alive, but he wasn't really living.

"Yes, it's difficult to see my mother sick, but it's more difficult to not have the only girl that I ever truly loved in my life right now." He gazed into my eyes, searching for an expression to see if I had any feelings that were mutual.

"I know that you care for me. That's great, but we aren't going to talk about me. We're going to discuss you and what you've been up to while we smash these wings and fries." I quickly changed the subject as I handed him his plate of food. The way he opened that plate and picked over those fries, I could tell that he wasn't really hungry. My guess was that he lied about being hungry, just so that he could have an excuse to see me that day.

"You really need to eat all of that food, I mean every single bite. You're still skinny as hell. You could use some meat on them bones." I laughed while licking the ranch dressing off my fingers. He was always bony as hell, so I had to be honest. Hell, sometimes I wondered if I was ever too much for him because of my thickness.

He placed his fingers on my face to show me how he was feeling at that moment, and I lifted up my hand to slide his hand right off of my face.

"Look, I appreciate the fact that you care, but I'm not ready for anything else right now," I explained as I finished the last wing on my plate and then wiped my hands with the napkins in my bag.

I looked back into his face, and I saw the disappointment as a tear rolled down his face. I have never known him to be sensitive, not in front of me, so he must have felt very weak at the moment.

"Look, Vonne, your mother is sick right now, so maybe you're searching for affection and comfort. Sometimes, when we go through a lot or something extreme, we tend to become vulnerable," I added as he stopped crying before he embarrassed himself.

"You're in a relationship with someone else; aren't you?" he asked, and I slowly nodded my head to let him know that I was. Vonne and I may have been broken up, but I always told him everything, and although I didn't want him to hurt the way he was, I had to ensure that I put myself first. Yes, it may sound a little selfish, but nobody can live my life but me, and when it's all said and done, I'm the only one who will dramatically pay for my awful decisions.

As soon as I was about to explain, his mother knocked on the door.

"Come in, Mama," he said. My palms began to get sweaty because I wasn't ready to meet his mother. I really didn't want her thinking that we were together or him thinking that we would be just because I met her.

"Hey, son. I was going to ask you what you wanted for dinner," she said as she looked at him and then looked at me to see who it was that was keeping his company.

"Thanks, Mom, but I've already have some food. Legacy brought me some chicken and fries. If you want me to get you something else I will, because I know you don't eat this." He stood up, thinking his mother was going to rush him out of the house to get her something to eat, but he got another reaction instead.

"Ohm you're Legacy; you look more beautiful in person. I have seen many pictures of you, and my son speaks highly of you all of the time," she said as she walked over to give me a hug. I stood up to hug her back, although I was slightly embarrassed. I was the girl who had broken his heart and walked out of his life. I was the reason that he moved from North Carolina back to Georgia, and he still spoke highly of me to his mother. I wasn't really shocked though because of the heart this man had.

After his mother hugged me, she felt the need to leave out of the room to give us some privacy. She also let her son know that she was feeling well enough to fix a TV dinner and that he should spend time with me before I left. We sat there and talked about everything, mostly about the things that I wanted to do with my life and how he had worked himself up at KFC until he got that manager's position he had spoken of when we were dating back in North Carolina. I spoke of my situation with Sydney and the things I went through, and then, I cried on his shoulder.

"Stay here with me; I will take care of you. You don't deserve to be hurt the way he has been hurting you. Just tell me what I did or didn't do, so I can fix it, Legacy. Please." He kissed my hands, and tears ran down his face again. I looked into his eyes, trying to find the words to say to him that wouldn't make the pain run even deeper than it already was.

"I can't be with you; we can only be friends. I am in way too deep with Sydney, and just being honest, you would only end up being a rebound. You are far too special to just be someone's rebound. There is a girl out there who is made just for you; sad to say, that girl isn't me. I think that right now, since Sydney and I are taking a break,. I want to be single and find myself. I truly hope you understand my decision." I looked into his eyes, and I began to cry as well. I felt bad that I had to hurt him that way, and I didn't want him to walk away as if he had lost his best friend. He was special, but he wasn't my future husband.

"Can't you stay with me for the night?" he asked, and I agreed. I didn't see anything wrong with spending time with him and catching up on things. Nightfall approached, and he gave me a t-shirt with some jogging pants to wear. It was very cold in their house because of the air being on high, or maybe it was just me because I was anemic.

He put one of my favorite movies in the DVD player called *Enough*. I loved that movie because it represented a woman who was extremely broken because of a man who she thought she loved. She had to get away from him and take her daughter just to live in safety. He stalked her, no matter where she and her daughter moved away to, and she finally built up the strength and courage to fight back. She couldn't end up dead, and she knew he was crazy enough to finish her off. She decided to finish him off and take his life so she could peacefully live hers.

Vonne began touching my thighs and kissing my neck. My body started to tremble because, although Sydney was sleeping with as many hoes he could lay his hands on, I was being faithful during our entire relationship. I started remembering what it felt like to be held by someone who didn't cheat, someone who was loyal, and someone who knew how to really love someone else. He kissed my neck, then he made his way down to my belly button. After that, he found himself between my legs, sucking the lips off of my pussy. It felt so good as he licked my pussy up and down and then stuck his tongue inside like there was a tasty surprise waiting in there for his mouth.

My legs ran from him as I moaned, but not too loud so that his mother would not hear me. He eased his way back up after sucking me dry for twenty minutes, and then, he just held me. That was the first time I had a man who had sucked the walls out of my pussy so good and didn't even bother to try and stick his dick inside me afterwards. That showed me that he wasn't selfish and that his only worry that night was making sure I was satisfied. I fell asleep in his arms, and for the first time in a long time, I felt secure. I knew right away that whatever I told this boy to do, he would do it in the hopes of keeping me in his life. Had he known that the only reason I walked out of his life was because I didn't feel protected, he would have spent the rest of his life standing in front of me so that I would stay unharmed.

The next morning, I awoke to the best smell ever. I walked into the kitchen, and it was a full course breakfast. He cooked bacon, scrambled eggs with cheese, buttered toast, and grits with butter and cheese. These were all of my favorites, and he knew that.

"All of this for me, huh?" I leaned over his shoulder to take in the amazing smell of the breakfast as my stomach started to make all kinds of noise, letting me know that I was starving.

"Yes, actually for the two most important women in my life." He looked over at me and gave me a kiss.

My phone began to ring, but I ignored it. I wasn't ready to talk to Sydney just yet; I just wanted to deal with him when I made it back to

North Carolina. Although I didn't have any plans on being with Vonne, or with any man, I still needed that time completely to myself to do whatever I wanted to do.

He fixed my plate and sat it in front of me with a glass of orange juice. I couldn't wait to dig in as he took his mother's plate to her room. She wasn't really a morning person, so from what he had told me, she always slept in late.

"This is so good, Vonne. You really outdid yourself this morning," I said, beginning to get full halfway through my meal.

Ring…Ring… The doorbell rang, and Vonne went and answered it. It was his close friend, Tommy; they had grown up together and were really close. Tommy was such a good friend that when Vonne wanted to move to North Carolina, he supported his decision instead of trying to give him a million selfish reasons why he should stay like most people did.

"What's up with ya, Vonne?" he asked, as he looked at the breakfast that Vonne cooked. It was almost as if he didn't see me, sitting there, at the table, for a split second because he was busy trying to fix some of the cheesy grits.

"Legacy, this is my best friend, Tommy, and Tommy, this is Legacy, the girl I told you about from North Carolina." Vonne introduced us as Tommy sat right across from me at the table.

"I know who she is; I mean, really, man. You talk about her so much that I know you wouldn't just have another girl over here." Tommy said, as he slid the cheesy grits into his mouth.

"Dang, I guess I'm popular around Decatur, huh?" I asked as I took a sip from the orange juice that taste like it was freshly squeezed with just a little bit of pulp in it.

"Man, my dude is in love with you. I haven't seen him have it bad for no girl since high school. That girl, Madison, broke his heart. Man, he worked just to pay for her to go to school. She took up cosmetology, and by the time he had finished paying her way through school, she broke up with him." Tommy's eyes widened as he basically told Vonne's life story. This was my first time hearing about Madison because Vonne had never mentioned her before. Ever.

"Man, I am right here in the room." Vonne made it clear that Tommy was talking a little too much about his situation. He looked as if he was hurt all over again, just hearing the story come from Tommy's mouth. I could tell that this girl had done a tremendous number on his heart.

"Look, Vonne, I really enjoyed spending time with you, but I really have to go. I need to checkout from the hotel room or pay for another day," I explained because the last thing I needed was them locking me out of my room with all of my belongings in there. It was around 8:30 A.M., and checkout time was at 11:00 A.M. With the traffic in Atlanta, I needed to leave super early just to get there.

"Look, I need to speak to you in private for a few minutes before you leave," Vonne said, and I was almost sure that whatever he had to say, he didn't want to say it around his friend, Tommy. Hell, with the mouth that Tommy had, he couldn't even hold water, so I didn't blame him.

"Okay, I have a few minutes to spare," I said as I got up from the table and placed my plate into the sink. I went and got my purse, and then, I went outside as Vonne followed behind me.

"Look, I really love you more than anything; I want you to stay with me, Legacy. You don't have to worry about a thing; I will take care of you. Just be mine again," he said as his eyes began to water.

"I know you will find the perfect girl one day. You have to be patient. Okay? And remember, you can call me whenever you need to talk to someone," I said, giving him a friendly kiss on his cheek and walking away from his house. I got into my car and went back to the hotel. I was ready to check out the hotel and drive back to North Carolina.

"Hello. I am going to check out this morning," I said to the receptionist after I got all of my things out of the hotel room. I reached for my keys over and then left. That four-hour drive was hard because the first stop for me was going to be to check up on Sydney. I knew deep down inside that we had issues. I didn't know if he would ever change, but spending that night with Vonne just made me realize that I craved for his heart, and he already had mine.

I had finally pulled up at his house, and I was going to get him to help me return my car to the rental dealership I had borrowed it from. As I pulled up, there was an unfamiliar car outside of his father's house right beside his. I wasn't sure who it was.

Knock…knock…knock…

I pounded on the door as I placed my other hand against the peephole.

My heart was racing, and my hands trembled. The door slowly opened, and I stood there, furious as hell. Tisha opened the door, and she was standing there with the 'bitch, I've been fucking your man' face, and I couldn't control myself.

Chapter 12: Loving Mr. Wrong

Tisha

I met Sydney when I was in high school. I was about to graduate, and so was he. I, along with the other girls who went there, admired his smile, I was a cheerleader, and he was somewhat of a nerd, and I had a child already. I had been stupid with one of the guys on the football team because we dated, and I allowed him to tell me he loved me one night after a game. Before you knew it, I was fucking him, right in the backseat of his car.

After that night, my reputation was severely damaged, and I knew that I would place my interest in a different kind of guy. I didn't like the way I felt being hurt, and it was not comforting at all, being a mother in high school. Randy was my first love; he was my first everything, but I guess his popularity had gotten the best of him. He claimed he wasn't ready to be a father when I told him I was pregnant, and then, a few days later, I saw him with my best friend, who was also a cheerleader, Vanna. I couldn't help but feel betrayed, so yes, I went for the smart guy, who never had a girl on his arms whenever I saw him, but who was sexier than he knew he was. That guy was always Sydney. Sydney accepted my daughter, and we ended up going our separate ways when it was time for graduation. He went off to college, and I got a job as a bank teller at BB&T to support my daughter, Riley.

"Baby, I thought you were coming over to see me today," I questioned. I wasn't sure what was going on with him in college; I just knew he had a set of new friends and never had time for me anymore. Maybe he felt the pressure of me being a mother and didn't want to raise someone else's child. I was built strong because my mother, Trinity, was a single mother of three children. I have two brothers, and she has always done what she needed to do to make sure we had everything we needed. I had fallen so deeply for Sydney because he knew everything about me. He wasn't cocky, and he wasn't a hoe. I was more than sure that there was an explanation when I went to his college dorm to see what had been going on.

As I got into the dorm, I heard a few females in there. I didn't even bother him because I was afraid to lose him. I went back to my two-bedroom apartment, and I cried my eyes out. I knew Sydney didn't like confrontation or drama, so I was always walking on thin ice, trying not to lose him. The words that came from my sexy dark lips, everything I said and did, I had to be careful about it. I had done everything I thought a woman was supposed to do to keep her man and to keep her man from being unfaithful. There wasn't a time I wouldn't give him these sweet juices from this pussy, and there definitely wasn't a time where I was afraid to stick all of his dick inside of my mouth.

I could tell he loved me, but he wasn't ready to love me all of the way because he had his whole life ahead of himself. I started having feelings of doubt. I started feeling like maybe I wasn't good enough - that was until he got arrested for some shit he didn't do. I was beyond hurt, but I knew that was my opportunity to be there for him like a real woman should. After the first few times I went to visit him, I started seeing another woman's name on the visitation sheet. I couldn't believe my eyes; Amira Lockhart was her name, and she was already there visiting him, so I couldn't see him that day. The more I kept going there to see him, the more I kept getting let down. One day, while I was walking in, she was walking out, and I knew it was her because she looked like me. She was pregnant as hell, and I had been with him long enough to know what type of women he was interested in. I stopped her in her tracks and asked - just to see what she would say.

"What's your name? You look really familiar," I asked as she stood there, rubbing her belly. She had to have been at least six months pregnant.

"I'm Amira, but I'm sure I don't know you from anywhere," she said as she ran her fingers through her long, jet black hair.

"You have been coming to see Sydney?" I asked, just to see her response. I already knew she had been coming to see him, but I wanted to know why and who she was to him.

"Yes, I have, but who are you?" she asked as she immediately went into defense mode.

"I'm his girlfriend, and who are you?" I asked, the look on her face turned from a curious one to a sad one.

"I'm his girlfriend and his baby's mother. As you see, I'm carrying his baby," she said, still rubbing her stomach and then rolling her eyes at me. I wanted to beat her ass right there in that prison, but I couldn't bring myself to do that because he had probably been lying to her, just like he was lying to me. I turned around and walked out of that prison that day, and tears flowed from my eyes, dropping all over the steering wheel while I sat in my car. I couldn't believe I had been such a fool, thinking he was going to commit with me. My self-esteem had been so low, and I didn't even bother to take Sydney's calls, but I had to move on and still do what I had to do for me and mine.

I went to work at the bank, as usual, and one Tuesday, at around 12:00, that's when it happened. This handsome, brown skinned guy named Randy walked in to make a deposit. I was his teller, and he kept complimenting me on how beautiful I was as he deposited $657.90. We exchanged numbers, which is something that I usually didn't do, and after that, the rest was history. A few years had gone by, and I had two children with Randy; I cared so much about him, but my feelings for Sydney never went away. When I found out that Sydney was being released from prison, I was over excited, and just like that, I had broken up with Randy and taken Sydney back.

I thought everything was fine because I immediately conceived my daughter, Rihanna, with Sydney, but when I had her, he became distant. He broke up with me when she was only three months old, and I had no clue as to why. I had heard rumors about some girl he was seeing because my family and friends would see them together all the time around town. I found out where they were actually at one day because my cousin was in the same hotel lobby when they were checking in. The next morning, when it was check out time, I was out there in the parking lot, waiting for them to come out. As soon as they came out and got into his car, I pulled up to block them from being able to leave.

In my head, I had gone over what I would say to them, but when I walked up to the car, I could only confront him because, when I took one look at this girl, I could see why he was so distant from me. She was drop dead gorgeous. She had slanted eyes, a pretty, caramel brown complexion, and everything about this girl was flawless. Her hair was fucked up, and that alone let me know that they had been fucking all night long, so I was hurt. That day, I had suicidal thoughts, and if it hadn't been for my children, I wouldn't even be here anymore. I started messing around with Randy, and nothing got to Sydney because he was obviously in love with this girl.

He never even took full responsibility for Amira when she was pregnant, but here he was, showing this girl off to all of his family and friends and taking up for her. I started to think her pussy was wrapped up in gold because, no matter what, he wouldn't stop fucking around with her. When other bitches confronted me in the past, he would leave their asses alone, but he never left her alone. I just didn't understand.

A few years later, my daughter was turning two years old, and she was talking pretty good. I enjoyed watching my babies grow up because they were all I had. The night before her second birthday party, I was sitting on my couch, doing her hair, and that's when it happened. The moment that would take your breath away, that moment that would completely piss off any mother.

"Mama, can I see my other mama tomorrow? Can she come to my party?" That's what my daughter asked me as I was braiding and putting beads in her hair.

"Baby, I'm your mama; you don't have another mom," I explained to her, so she would understand that.

"I do have another mommy; her name is Legacy," she explained, and that was the moment that I stopped doing my baby's hair, and we left, heading to Sydney's father's house. I had my baby in my arms, and I banged on the door, ready to slap the fuck out of him. He answered the door and came outside as if he was nervous and shocked to see me.

I put my daughter down and slapped the shit out of him right there.

"Mommy, please don't hurt Daddy!" My daughter screamed out as tears ran down her little face.

"Why in the fuck would you have my daughter calling that bitch, Legacy, mama?" I asked. I stood there as the rain began to fall, waiting for his response. I wanted him to say some shit that I didn't like because I was ready to slap the fuck out of him.

"I never had my daughter calling her mama; I don't know what the fuck you're talking about, and you need to come in so my daughter doesn't get sick, standing in the damn rain," he said in his calmest voice, and I grabbed my daughter's hand and followed him inside.

"Well, she asked me if her other mama can come to her party tomorrow!" I stared into his eyes to see the reaction he would have.

"Man, I never meant to hurt you; I can't help that they are close. You have to respect that because I have moved on, and you need to move on, too," he said to me. That was okay because, as I looked around the house, his girl was obviously nowhere around. I was going to see if he had truly moved on; I was going to put his so called loyalty to the test.

"Well, we need to stay for the night because it looks like the roads are too bad." I stared into his gorgeous eyes as my daughter made her way to the room.

"Okay, you can stay. She has some clothes in the room, so Y'all can take baths, and I will get you a t-shirt and boxers to sleep in," he said as he walked away to do exactly as he said he would.

He got me a polo t-shirt, some polo boxers, and a pair of his polo socks for me to wear. This man was obsessed with name brand clothing. All the time I had been with him, and I had never seen him in anything that wasn't by a popular brand. I gave my daughter a bath, and then, I took a shower as he put our daughter to sleep while I was in the tub. I left out of the bathroom, with nothing on but a towel, and I walked into his bedroom and dropped the towel. I wanted to show off every inch of my sexy, chocolate body. As he stared at me, I waited for him to say something.

"Aren't you going to say anything?" I asked after I stood there for a minute while he stayed quiet.

"Put some clothes on; your blanket and pillow are waiting for you on the couch," he said to me as he sat on the bed with a smirk on his face. He was so got damn arrogant, and the same thing that once attracted me was now such a turn off.

I put on the white polo shirt, the blue and white polo boxers, and whit polo socks and then stomped my way to the living room. I laid on the couch as tears covered my face for a while. I cried quietly to myself because I didn't want any pity. I wanted him to want me because he loved me, not because we had a daughter together and damn sure not because he felt sorry for me. I laid on the couch, snuggled up in that blanket, and fell asleep.

The next morning, when I awakened, I didn't even say a damn word to this asshole I called my child's father as I got myself and my daughter dressed and got ready to leave his father's house. As soon as I put my shoes on, there were knocks that were so loud on the door that you would have thought that it was the police coming to take his ass to jail or something. I looked out the peephole, but I didn't see a face, so I continued to open up the door. It was no surprise that Legacy was standing there, looking pissed as fuck.

Chapter 13: Infatuated with Skrilla

Legacy

I saw red as I stood there, looking at this stupid ass bitch in her face. Out of all bitches that he could have been fucking with, he chose to fuck with her while I was away. Yes, I had spent a few days with Vonne and all, but I didn't fuck the nigga, so I didn't do anything wrong by letting him nibble on my juicy pussy. The look on her face told it all as I yanked the bitch by her mothafuckin hair and dragged her ass right there on Skrilla's dad's front porch. My fingernails engraved her dark-skinned face as she struggled to fight back and get some hits in as well. Skrilla ran outside and attempted to pull me off her, but I reached up and slapped his ass while I had a fistful of her weave in my other hand.

"Baby, please stop. Let me explain!" Skrilla yelled as he continued to try and pull me off of her. All I wanted to do at that very moment was get that bitch ready for her own funeral, and then, there was a voice that stopped it all.

"Please don't hurt my mommy, Legacy. Please!" Rihanna cried out as she came out of the door and watched us fight like hell. I instantly dropped my fist and let go of her hair, and then, she jumped up and grabbed her daughter off the porch.

"It was storming, so she stayed over. She slept on the couch," he explained as she stood there with their daughter in her arms.

"Why in the hell should I believe you, Sydney? I loved you, and this is how you repay me?" I screamed out as sweat rolled down my face, and my eyes turned bloodshot red. Before he could even say anything, I jumped back into the car and pulled off. I looked into my rearview window and saw him right behind me, but I didn't give a damn. My cellphone started to ring back to back, and I knew it was him, so I didn't answer. After I saw that he wasn't going to stop following me, I finally answered his calls to see what in the hell he possibly could have to say to me.

"What in the hell do you want?" I screamed out in his ear.

"Baby, meet me at my mama's house," he said, and although I was hesitant about it, I followed him over there anyway.

When we arrived at his mama's house, I got out, and he dropped to his knees, trying to beg for my forgiveness.

"Baby, I don't want anything to do with her; I promise. I just want you and my daughter; that is all," he said as he grabbed my hand, while he was on his knees, right there in front of his mother's house on her lawn.

"After everything I have done for you. I have stayed by your side, I hid your dope in my pussy, so you wouldn't go back to jail, I have helped you bag that shit up. I have dealt with your dumb ass groupies, who don't take no for an answer, and out of all bitches, you run back to your baby's mama. You said she wasn't shit, you said she was an unfit mother, and you had me helping you raise your daughter. I love your daughter, and I'm attached to her as if she was my own, but you won't use that to try and hurt me, thinking I'm gonna just sit around and be a main chick dummy!" I yelled as I took a rubber band out of my purse to place my Brazilian weave into a ponytail.

"I promise on everything I love, on my grandfather in his grave, that I did not touch that girl," he said as his eyes became watery. Right then and there, I could tell he was telling the truth because, if he had stuck his dick in the girl, he definitely wouldn't have lied on his late grandfather. It was clear that he didn't want to lose me, and it was even clearer that the bitch spent the night to try and break us up. I had once played all those games before, I was once a player, so you can't try tricks on the person who invented the mothafuckin game. I was happy that I beat her ass, and I could only imagine how she felt when she saw him chase after me, instead of consoling her. He was mine, and I loved him with all of my heart; I knew he was no good, but I couldn't just let him go. I knew he was fucking around; he just tried his best to cover his tracks, but I still wasn't ready to call it off with him. I was in love with this man's dirty draws, I was drawn in by his pearly white smile, and I was infatuated with this man's whole being.

"You have to promise me that you will cut off any bitches that you have and be loyal to me," I mumbled as tears began to flow down my face.

"I promise you don't have to worry about that type of shit anymore, Legacy." He begged and pleaded as he got off of his knees and wrapped his arms around my waist.

"I have been through so much shit in my life. I have been abused by my mother and was told I was never gonna be shit. I need you to be more supportive of me trying to be independent, and stop thinking that I'm trying to get ahead, just so I can leave you," I hugged him, reassuring him that as long as he was my backbone then I would be his. We went into his mother's house, and we made passionate love in the middle of the day while everyone else was either at school or still at work.

My pussy walls tightened over his dick, and I began to scream out as my eyes rolled to the back of my head. His dick made me wanna cry; it felt so fuckin good inside of me. Every time we fucked, it was like the slate was clean and clear. My ass jiggled as he fucked me doggy style, and he slapped my ass until my ass cheeks turned red.

We fucked all day long - in his bed, in his shower, hell, even on his mother's couch. When we were finished, he had something he wanted to talk about, so I laid with him in his bed as he told me whatever he had to tell me.

"Baby, I have been saving up money, and I want us to find a house together," He said as he laid there, butt ass naked, comforting my naked, caramel toned body.

"Oh my gosh; so, you're really ready to do this?" I asked because I was ready and glad he was ready to make that move with me as well. He hadn't ever lived with a woman before; even when he was with Tisha, he was still back and forth to his parents' houses, so he never took everything he owned over there. I was happy about his decision, and I told him yes.

I laid there in his bed, kissing him and staring into his eyes, happy that we were taking a step forward. I wasn't sure he would change his life completely, but only time could tell. As we laid there, I thought about everything that had happened in my life and how I was going to fix everything.

"Baby, I have been through so much, and I have so many dreams. I want to go back to school, find a good job, and get my daughter back," I explained. His eyes grew big because, although I had mentioned my daughter, London, I had never gone into details because the pain of it all was still burned very deep.

"Baby, we will take one step at a time, and you know a nigga's got you. Shit, I need to move these bricks and shit and make shit happen," he explained, and then, all of a sudden, shots fired outside. He pulled out his 40-caliber pistol, right before there was a kick on the door.

hug, you have to be ready to kill for him, ready to protect your life, and pull that trigger.

Damn it's not as fun as it seems being caught up with a real nigga.

Chapter 14: He's Mine

Legacy

I jumped out of the bed to see what the noise was that was coming from the door. It didn't sound like knocks; instead, it sounded like someone was kicking the door. I leaned my head around the corner, preparing for the worst, all the while, I repeated in my head, *This is what you signed up for when you chose to be with Skrilla.'* He looked out of the peephole, ran right afterwards; he lowered his gun as if he knew who the person on the other side was.

"Damn, nigga, don't do that shit," he said as he gave his cousin a handshake. It was Malcom; he didn't deal with Malcom all of the time, but when he did, you always knew there was big money involved. They were really good friends, but at the same time, they both were always busy, trying to stack paper.

"I'm sorry, nigga, but it's hot out tonight. Hell, some young niggas up the street are having a damn standoff with the police right now. That shit is going on at the end of your street," he said as he took his gun out of his pants and placed it on the table. He looked shook, not because there was a standoff was going on, because real niggas were always used to shit like that, but only because his ass didn't want to be locked up.

"Man, next time you need to call. I told you I was about to put a bullet up your ass," Skrilla said. He was waving his gun from side-to-side while he was talking to Malcom, right before he placed his gun on the table, right beside Malcom's gun.

"Man, I would have called if I planned on stopping by. Hell, I just needed to sit here for a while until that shit outside cools down and them damn police officers go about their business. A nigga ain't trying to get arrested tonight; hell, I'm supposed to be getting some pussy from this bad bitch that's in town for the weekend." Malcom sat down in one of the chairs at the kitchen table, making himself at home.

"Hell, nigga, what do you think I was trying to do? Shit, my girl is here," Skrilla said as he waved his hand, letting me know I needed to come on out of the room and say hello to his cousin, Malcom.

"Hey, Malcom. How are you doing?" I asked as I strutted towards the kitchen with Skrilla's Polo t-shirt on and some shorts I had slipped on to cover my bottom.

"Shit. I'm doing fine but not as fine as you," he said to me. Then he looked at Skrilla and said, "I hope you don't lose this one; she's the baddest one you've ever had. Hell, I bet all of your exes are mad as hell, hating on her." He started laughing as he pulled out some money and put it on the table to count it up.

"My nigga, they're mad as hell. They be hating like hell on my baby; shit, even Rihanna's mama be doing dumb shit and lying, trying to make her leave me." Skrilla looked at me and smiled with the brightest smile, trying to show me that what he said was a compliment.

I walked over to Skrilla, gave him a kiss, and then went back into his room. I had contemplated leaving him on many occasions, but I guess the love I had for him was so strong that it somehow made me want to risk my life for it all. I know; who would want to risk their life over a man, right? Well, the kind of woman who is loyal and takes the love she gives out very seriously; that's who. I hadn't heard from Vonne since I left Atlanta. He tried to call me a few times, but I guess he gave up on me. I think deep down inside that's what I wanted to happen. I wasn't strong enough to choose between the two, so someone had to eventually go. Skrilla sat in the kitchen with his cousin, Malcom, while I sat on the bed, flipping through channels on the television, as thoughts still arose about our relationship and where it was going. We had been together for two years, and we still weren't living together. I was more than ready to make that huge step and get a place of our own together.

"Alright, my nigga. I'll see you later." Malcom gave Skrilla a hug, and then he left.

Skrilla walked into the room and sat on the bed. I had finally decided to watch CSI MIAMI because it had always been one of my favorite shows.

"Hey, baby, there's something I need to talk to you about," I said as I contemplated on what I would say and how I would say it to him.

"What's up, baby?" he asked as he placed his hands on my thigh.

"I want to know when we will start looking for a place of our own; I'm ready for us to live together," I said as I looked into his eyes to search his soul and find some sort of confirmation of his feelings.

"Let me guess. You're gonna ask a nigga to have a baby with you and put a ring on your finger next, huh?" he said in the most aggravated manner ever. I felt disgusted by his choice of words. Hell, after two years, I would think I deserved all of that plus more.

"Hell, yes; I deserve that. I shouldn't have to ask for those type of things. Hell, you have me raising your daughter, but I can't have a baby of my own by you? You've got me risking my freedom, and probably my damn life each day I'm with you, and being your wife is too much to ask? Fuck outta here, Sydney!" I screamed at him as I jumped up off the bed and started grabbing my belongings. He jumped up behind me and grabbed my arm, as if he wasn't going to allow me to leave.

"Baby, please don't go," he said as I hesitated for a moment, and tears started flowing from my eyes.

"Look, your baby mama may have settled with being your girlfriend for over a decade, but you should know by now that I'm not that kind of girl. I'm the kind of girl that you should wife, and if you don't, there's always a line of niggas waiting patiently behind for you to fuck up!" I shouted as I yanked my arm back from him.

"Well, go have them niggas then. I bet you'll never meet a nigga like me anyway!" he shouted as he sat back on the bed as if he didn't give a damn about me leaving. I was tired of placing my heart in this nigga's hands, only for him to slam it on the ground and step on that shit repeatedly, as if it didn't mean a damn thing to him. I wasn't going to sit around and play house with a nigga who didn't see himself in a long-term commitment, which went past being boyfriend and girlfriend. Since I was a little girl, I had dreamed about my dream wedding, my future husband, and most of all, having little babies of my own.

I was in too deep, and I couldn't stand the thought of losing him, no matter how much we argued and didn't see eye to eye, but I was always down to teach him a little lesson. I left, and I went to a friend's house. Her name was Jessabelle. She was a very pretty, light-skinned girl with a slim waist and fat ass. She always drew attention, just like I did, everywhere she went.

"What's up, Legacy? What's wrong? Why are you looking sad? You better not tell me Skrilla ain't acting right because I will surely murder his ass myself," she said as she scrambled her eggs with bacon. So many people in the hood loved eating breakfast for dinner, hell even after they left the club. It just was our type of thing.

"Hell, he's been tripping. Shit a bitch gets tired of riding or dying for a nigga who can't even get his shit together," I stared at her and tried my best not to feel embarrassed. I couldn't believe I was sitting here even talking about him not having his shit together at this point.

"Bitch, what you need to do is teach that nigga some discipline; he will get his shit together." She took a sip of her Moscato and sat down beside me.

"All niggas ever need is some act right, and they will eventually man up right." I agreed, as I took my shoes off and got comfortable. Jessabelle's house was laid; she danced at a local strip club for a living. The only thing I didn't like was that the bitch had different niggas running in and out of her crib. Some nigga came out of her bedroom with nothing on but some boxers and a wife beater to get some damn apple juice out of the fridge.

"Well, are you going to sit around, or are you going to get a blanket out of the hallway closet?" she asked as she admired the ass on the dark chocolate eye candy that she flaunted around her crib.

"I think I'm going to go Jessabelle. Besides, it looks like you are kind of tied up tonight. Thanks for the food and for letting me vent a little though." I got up and gave her a hug before leaving her house. As soon as I walked out of the house, some nigga was walking up to the door.

"Is Jessabelle up in there? Whose car is this in the damn driveway?" he asked, looking mad as hell, like he was about to lash out.

"I don't know anything about that; I've got to go now. Nice seeing ya," I said, right before I got into my car. I drove off thinking, *'Damn, my girl must have that bomb pussy like me.'*

I went back to his house and thought about going in, but then I didn't. I decided to go to my aunt's house and stay for a little while. It was almost three o'clock in the morning; luckily, I had a spare key for whenever I needed to crash at her house. I eased my way into the house and went to take a shower. My aunt was sound asleep; she must had smoked a fat blunt. Everyone around me always smoked and drank, so that was always normal because that was what I always saw. My body was drenched, yet I smelled like a million bucks when I walked into the spare bedroom at my aunt's home that belonged to me. I dropped my towel to the floor, and then I realized some pervert was peeping at me through my damn window.

"What the fuck do you want?" I realized it was Skrilla, so I picked the towel back up, wrapped my body with it, and then went to the front to open the door.

"Baby, why didn't you come back home?" he asked as he walked right on in like I invited his ass in or some shit.

"Look, I'm not that girl. Okay? I done told you so many fucking times that I will not chase not a got damn soul. If you don't want to get your shit together, I'm not the one for you. I'm completely positive that I don't have any more got damn time to waste on you period!" I walked back to the room as he followed. He came in and closed the door.

"Look, baby, I will do whatever you want me to do; I just need some time. You know how a nigga feels about moving in with a female. I told you the last time I tried that shit, it didn't work out." He walked over to me and grabbed my body. I loved this man's got damn touch, the way he breathed, the things he said - or maybe it was just how he said them. I loved his swagger, his style, and grace. I loved the got damn ground he walked on. By this time, so many people thought I was fucking stupid for loving him. It was no secret that we were dating and that we were serious, but his reputation was no secret either. My biggest fear had always been being lied to, and I just couldn't take anymore hurtful surprises.

"You are still fucking around with this bitch and that bitch. I bet you still fuck your baby mama too; that bitch doesn't have any reason to play on my phone. Hell, who knows who it could be? After all, your dick is wrapped in gold or some shit, right?" I asked him as he yanked the pink towel off my body and turned me over, placing my ass right up in the air and spreading my ass cheeks apart so he could get on his knees and lick my ass from the back.

"Damn, baby," he mumbled with his mouth full of pussy; my pussy must have tasted like strawberries with the way he moaned. You would have thought the nigga was eating some Krispy Kreme doughnuts that were hot and ready.

My pussy was like nourishment, and he treated it as such. He stood up, after slurping the juices that splashed from my pussy onto his lips, unbuckled his pants, and slid his long, fat dick right inside of me.

"Fuck yes!" I moaned and yelled as he went back and forth, left to right, hitting each and every part of me that I didn't know was there. The man had skills, and if there were any walls hiding up in there, he knew all the right strokes to perform in order to find them. My pussy gripped on his long, fat dick as he began to moan louder and louder. He came right inside of me, which was the best sex period. The kind of sex where you didn't give a damn about who heard you or who was watching. The kind of sex that made you want to have that nigga's baby. He always took me there, and maybe for that reason alone, I just could never let go. I fell out onto the bed and crawled up, just like a baby. Before you knew it, the sun was rising, and so was Skrilla's dick.

"Get up, baby," he said as he rubbed his python up and down, as if he was ready to go right then and there.

"Look, nigga, we ain't about to have sex this morning. I'm still burned out from last night." I rolled my eyes and then smiled, giving him both personalities at once.

"For real though, baby; let's go. I've got a surprise for you." We both got up, and we left. We got on the highway and kept riding. I was curious as to where he was taking me, but I didn't ask. I knew that once he had his mind set on something, that was it, and obviously, he didn't want me to know just yet. He played Drake and Jeezy, his two favorite rappers, for the whole ride to Myrtle Beach, South Carolina, and I was excited. We arrived there after only an hour and a half because he drove fast as hell; often, his driving scared me. I always thought that stepping into his car could be the last time I took a ride. When we arrived, I couldn't believe how beautiful it was. The ocean was spectacular, just mind blowing. Looking into his eyes and holding his hand as we pulled up to the hotel room, I knew I had made the right decision. Sometimes, we go through shit with our men; all the ladies understand what I'm talking about, but when you love someone, I mean truly love them, there's no turning back from that shit. Ultimately, your heart can't help who it loves. What so many people didn't realize was that, yes, Sydney was a thug, but hell, thugs had feelings too. They bleed the same blood that everyone else bleed, and when people weren't around, they cried the same damn tears. Hustling had always been his focus; money made the world go around, but he needed love. Every thug needed a real woman in his life. I kissed his soft red lips; that kiss had always been everything and more. He ran his fingers through my hair and then got out of the car to open my door for me.

"Thank you, baby; I appreciate that." I smiled at his gorgeous red face, forgetting all the pain he had put me through. I may have been a fool in love again, but as long as I had him, nothing else mattered.

"You deserve it. Shit, I've done a lot of shit, and you still stick with me. I don't wanna keep fucking shit up with us, so I gotta show you that I can be the man you need me to be." Skrilla pulled up his baggy pants to keep his Polo boxers from showing as we made our way into the hotel. I leaned on him as we checked into the reserved hotel room. His smell... oh, how I loved that damn scent that drew me in each and every time. When he was away, I always had an extra t-shirt of his that had his scent lingering on it that I would put under my nose, close my eyes, and imagine he was still right there with me.

We made our way into the hotel room. I looked around and admired the beautiful oceanfront view; all the while, I didn't notice he wasn't worried about the view because he had his eyes on me the whole time. He turned me around so that my focus wouldn't be on the ocean view; it'd be on only him. He grabbed my ass, with his big strong hands, and pulled me in closer.

"Nobody's gonna do you like me," I said as I tongue kissed every inch of his mouth. I wanted him to indulge in the taste of my lips, so I wore cherry flavored lip-gloss just for him.

"I've got what you need, baby. Take these clothes off," he whispered in my ear. Those words made me feel good, made me feel like I had just hit the lottery, and I was definitely banking with him. We quickly undressed, and he started pleasing me from my head down to my toes. He knew how to work that tongue; you'd think that every inch of my body was like eating a bowl of the sweetest fruit because of the faces he made while he tasted every inch of my skin, until he went straight for the juices. He got on his knees and started sucking my toes, and I moaned so loudly that my voice placed a trembling effect in his face. The way his dick felt inside of me sent chills down my spine. My knees were slightly bent over the bed as the pounds came back to back. I moaned louder and louder, the more he shoved his big dick inside of me, and although he had taken me to such a beautiful place, nothing else mattered because there was no thoughts of the beautiful beach in my mind. When we were finished, we laid together, and we loved on each other in every way possible.

Every day we spent at the beach together was like a walk in the park for me.

He took me to Ripley's Believe It or Not, the aquarium, and out to eat at an all you can eat buffet. We were like two big kids on vacation, and the only moments we spent in the room were to make love.

I fell in love with his ass more and more each day, and there was no way I could have been caught because of how fast I fell. We walked together on the beach at night, with me wearing only my two-piece. He told me that moment reminded him of the first night we met, when I went for a swim at night in the hotel and got caught. He slowly took my two-piece off, pulled his dick out, laid my body on the sand, and fucked me right there on the beach. I didn't know if it felt good because he had some good sex, or if it was the fact we were doing it out in public, and we could have been caught.

Our last days at the beach were like magic; the clock was ticking faster, and I didn't want to let that moment we shared go. We checked out of the room and stood on the beach, enjoying the water and the sun one last time before we got in his car and left.

We drove back home after enjoying our time away from all the drama. No nagging ass baby mama, no side hoes, no junkies cutting into our time - just him and I. Before you knew it, our trip to the beach was coming to an end, and our reality was starting to settle in. I had to go back home and deal with possibly getting into fights over him, because the fact that he was a ladies man would never change, and he had to go back home and make money in the streets, which was the best way he knew how.

We cruised down the highway, heading home. I tried to act like I didn't want him to go, so I started rubbing his dick and kissing him, as if I didn't care about us getting into a wreck, because he had lost focus of the road and what was ahead. His phone continued to ring for our entire ride home, and he didn't answer, so I automatically knew that he didn't want to talk to whoever was on the other line - or at least not in front of me.

We made it back safety, and just when I thought the surprise process was over, he had another one waiting for me. We pulled up in this nice neighborhood and parked in front of a nice house. It was brick, one level, and looked new.

"Baby, where are we?" I asked as I gazed into his dreamy eyes. He pulled out a blunt and lit it as he prolonged explaining why we were there.

"This our new crib. I mean, you have been bugging a nigga about stepping up. Shit, this is me stepping up right here. I hope you're grateful because can't no other woman say she done lived with me. Hell, I done had cribs in other bitches' names, and they couldn't even stay up in the places, regardless if their names were on the lease or not," Skrilla explained with bass in his voice. This was a huge step for him, and I didn't take it for granted. I didn't waste any time getting situated in our new place, gathering all my belongings from my aunt's and mother's places, and turning our house into a home. All I had to do was stay at home and hold shit down, and he would take care of the rest. Plenty of sleepless nights were ahead for me; little did I know because I couldn't sleep without my nigga. I assumed he was hustling to pay the bills, not worried that he was laying up with other bitches. I always got the dick when I wanted, so there really was nothing different, other than the fact that we were more serious than ever, and everyone knew about us.

"I'm so happy that we made this step together. I mean, I love this house. I can definitely see us starting a family here and being here for the long run." I sipped on a glass of red wine as I admired our house. I had been in just about every furniture outlet in Charlotte to make sure our crib was laid. Decorating had always been my strong point, plus I didn't know too many men who were good at decorating like women were anyway. My bathrooms looked like an islands. I was always infatuated with the islands, almost like I was an island girl in my first life. My shower curtains had the ocean on them, and they were reversible. My flat screen televisions were mounted on the walls, and the color theme was dark blue and black. I had always felt like the outcast in anything I was involved in, and that was why I was attracted to the color black.

"I'm happy if you're happy. Shit, this house wasn't cheap, none of this stuff in here was, but I'd do anything to make you smile, baby." He kissed me on my cheek as I placed my glass of wine on the counter to fix some chicken salads for us.

"You make me happy; keep making me happy and you will never have to worry about seeing the bitch in me." I made sure we were on the same page, finished fixing up our food, and we called it a night with our bellies on full.

Chapter 15: Secrets of A Real Nigga

Skrilla

My main focus was to get to the money and never change. Shit, there was so much shit Legacy didn't know about. I really didn't wanna move into a place with her, but I didn't want to lose her either. My parents were tripping about a nigga coming in and out of their shit all kinds of hours of the night, and my daddy's door being kicked in by the Feds didn't help either. No, they didn't find shit, except a petty ass bag of weed, and I wasn't even there. My daddy wouldn't give a nigga up, so they arrested him, and I had to drop a stack to bail him out of jail. I think I was at the point where I didn't think I would ever get tired of living the way I did. The fast life was so addictive, and it was hard as hell to shake. Many nights I didn't come home, and I knew Legacy stayed up, waiting on a nigga. Keeping it one hundred, I stayed laid up with different hoes when I get bored in the midst of making money. On the other hand, there was my baby mama, Tisha, who wouldn't stay off a nigga's dick. She was always complaining about some shit, and matters got worst when she somehow had one of her bitch ass friends find Legacy on Facebook, and she saw the pictures Legacy posted with us at the beach. Every real nigga knew how that shit goes. She started calling my phone late at night crying and shit, begging for a nigga to come over. She was asking me if I loved my girl and whether I still loved her or not.

"What are you doing? You took her to the beach, Sydney. How could you do that to me? You know how much I love you. I gave you ten fucking years of my life, and this is how you repay me? You know I had your child - not her. I was there for you when your brother died - not her! I was there for you when you didn't have shit, when you were on the come up. It was me there for you when you got another girl pregnant and when you were locked up, Sydney! I had to face that bitch while you were in prison. I looked at her belly when she was in her third trimester! How long will you put me through this shit, Sydney? I can't take this anymore, Syd," she cried over the phone. I heard everything she was saying, but I had no remorse.

"Maybe if you stop listening to your friends and shit, you wouldn't be so hurt. The same bitches who screenshot shit and are sending it to you are the same bitches who used to try and fuck me behind your back and shit. Tell me something, Tisha. Why the fuck are you worrying about me? You need to be worrying about getting them fake ass friends out of your got damn circle, going to work every day, and being a good mother to your kids!" I finally flipped out. I had become tired of this shit. I loved the chase but only if it was me doing the chasing. There was nothing that turned me off more than a weak ass woman who chased around niggas. Legacy was the first woman I met, that I was afraid to lose, who didn't stalk me. Shit, I had to stalk her, if anything, and that was one quality that made me fall in love with her. She was better looking in my eyes; she didn't walk around here getting pregnant and shit. And while Tisha was acting like she had amnesia, I damn sure didn't. Hell, she had two kids by other niggas, and here she was, throwing what I did with my dick in my face.

Tisha kept begging and begging a nigga; that shit seemed like it went on forever. That shit was annoying as hell; it was like a child crying for some shit in the store that they knew you weren't gonna buy.

I guess she realized a nigga wasn't falling for that shit, so she started threatening me, telling me that I wouldn't be able to see Rihanna anymore. She knew how I was about my daughter, and yet she wanted to threaten to take my daughter away for good. A nigga wanted to kill her stupid ass for that shit. I found myself having to fuck with the bitch, just to see my baby, hoping that shit wouldn't get back to Legacy. Once I did that shit, it made it easier for me to fuck any and everybody else. I wasn't afraid anymore; it was like breaking ice and shit. No matter who I fucked, I couldn't help but think about Legacy because she was the only woman who could fully satisfy me. It would take ten bitches to add up to one of Legacy, so what was the point of letting her walk out of a nigga's life? I had been drinking Lean and popping ecstasy pills, and living the fast life was like taking candy from a toddler; the shit was easy as hell. My pockets stayed fat, and I had all the clientele I needed because my crack made all the junkies come back. Going to the mall and balling out on Polo and Lacoste was nothing. A nigga could buy out the mall and still pay the bills on time. Nothing could bring me down, and nothing could stop me. As far as Legacy, I knew I could trust her with my life. She wouldn't hurt anybody; she was harmless. I didn't have to worry about her giving a nigga away to the Feds; I knew deep down inside she would die for a nigga. All I had to continue to do was play my cards right, and I wouldn't get caught up.

"Wake that ass up! Daddy's home." I smacked Legacy's ass as she pretended to yawn and roll over as if she had been in a deep ass sleep, and I had woken her up from a good dream. That was how she did every night. It didn't take a rocket scientist to know she stayed up every night, waiting on a nigga. She always wore some different type of lingerie with that pretty, brown ass sticking out of them thongs, slightly hanging on the side of the bed, with the blanket halfway down her legs. She would have perfume all over her body, the mild kind from Victoria's Secret, because she knew those strong ass fragrances always made me have allergic reactions.

"Hey, baby. I made dinner and put a plate up in the microwave. I missed you so much," she said as she sat up with titties hanging out of her shirt and looking like a stallion as always. I couldn't help but lick them juicy ass thighs. Then, before you knew it, a nigga was eating the box and slanging dick left to right.

She loved every bit of that shit, moaning all loud and looking back at a nigga while I hit it from the back; that shit always turned a nigga on. I was on cloud nine after we finished fucking. She lit a cigarette; I couldn't stand the smell because I didn't smoke cigarettes, but I tolerated it because I loved her. I lit a blunt, so I could feel as high as the clouds until I got hungry. I went to get my plate that she made me, ate the food, and went to sleep. That was the usual night, and although it never stopped her from questioning a nigga, she always forgave me in advance. Every morning I got up, just like I was going to a regular job, to hit the corner again and get to the money. My regulars had my pockets on fleek. I was getting paid, and little did Legacy know, I had two hundred thousand dollars saved up already.

I'd always been a smart ass nigga. Most niggas thought with their dicks and didn't have a brain to back that shit up, but I wasn't like that at all.

As far as Tisha… well, we would be good as long as she continued to play her position and stop using my daughter as a fucking pawn. We would be more than great. She already got all the money she wanted out of a nigga on a daily, but I guess that wasn't enough as long as my heart belonged to Legacy. I should have known that she would do whatever she could in order to fuck my relationship up. If she couldn't get me to break shit off with Legacy, she was going to go through Legacy herself and try to cause disaster by any means necessary.

I never knew I could be in this deep, but at this point, what more could a nigga do to get in more shit?

Chapter 16: Matter of Time

Tisha

I walked across the soft carpet of my four-bedroom home, which accommodated my children and I comfortably. I hadn't moved on much since it was officially over between Sydney and I; it wasn't because I didn't want to, but I didn't know how. He was my first love, and what hurt more than anything was feeling deep down inside that the love of your life left you, and it felt like he upgraded. I started to truly feel insecure, and the more time rolled by, the closer the two became. There were plenty of times that I watched them from a distance, without them knowing I was watching; hell, they didn't even know I knew they were staying together. Shit, it hurt deep as hell, and I couldn't help but look in the mirror and wonder what he saw in her that he did not see in me. I knew I wondered about that shit when they first got together, like any other woman would, but at the same damn time, I couldn't help but want to find out exactly what it was. The love that I once felt started growing into hatred as I realized that he just wasn't coming back. It took a long time for me to realize that, and no matter the evidence, I still was never convinced of the fact.

"Mommy, where's my daddy?" our daughter asked, while sitting on the edge of her bed and playing with one of her toys. I wanted to tell her badly that he wasn't coming back because he had a new leading lady in his life. No matter how badly I wanted to badmouth him to his daughter, like so many other baby mamas out there, I just couldn't bring myself to do that because he had always been a damn good father to her.

I often found someone to watch my children while my best friend and I hit up some of the best after spots to get drunk and forget about all of our damn problems.

"Girl, I know you're not still tripping off Skrilla. That nigga is going to be a nigga. Shit, he is a trap nigga at that! Didn't I tell you things would end up like this?" The music was playing loud as hell, but I could clearly hear what Serenity was saying. She had always been my best friend, and she always kept it a little too real. I couldn't deny the fact that she was absolutely right; I just didn't want to hear that shit at all. I dreamed about this man at night, and he was always the first thing on my mind when I woke up in the morning. I couldn't just move, so no matter who told me to do so, it'd just go in one ear and out the other.

"It's not the time for that shit, Serenity. I love you because you have always been there for me, but you don't know the half of what I am going through right now." I took another sip of my Long Island Iced Tea and slammed the glass back down on the table, almost causing the glass to shatter into pieces. The bartender looked at me like I was crazy. We were black women partying at bars with mostly Caucasian individuals, and it was sad to say that black folks didn't always have a good time without fights breaking out and gun shots ringing in your ear. Not discrediting my people whatsoever, but white folks knew how to have a good ass time. There were kegs, and what alcoholic didn't love to drink alcohol beverages out of barrels? The bartender was damn near racist, and me slamming glasses across the damn bar didn't help any.

"You need to calm down, and I know enough! I know he left you for someone younger than you. The girl probably can't even go in the ABC Store and buy her own bottles. Probably can't even work the muscles in her kiddie pussy yet," she mumbled.

"She is doing something right. I just want to know what the fuck it is," I replied with a tone that showed I had lost all hope. I didn't know what to do at that point, so I allowed the drinks to bring me comfort. Comfort I couldn't find myself, I thought. I left the bar so fucking drunk that I couldn't even drive; I called an Uber. On the way to my house, I reminisced about the times Sydney and I shared. I thought of how good it felt when his nine-inch dick was deep inside of me. Back then, when I used to get drunk with my girls, I knew I could come home to Sydney, and it turned me on. I loved the way it felt when I would go out with my girls; all the niggas in the club would try to get with us, but I'd tell them I had a man and go home to him. That was the best sex to me, and when we were finished, I'd fall straight to sleep and wake up to breakfast in bed. It was the little shit he did; you know? Get a bitch's mind, and the rest would come along was the strategy of a clever nigga, and he did just that. When I got home, I took a shower to wash the sweat off my body, and then laid in my bed to watch *The Keyshia Cole Show*. I loved Keyshia; her music seemed to get me through tough times whenever Sydney would break my heart, so when she came out with a show, I definitely didn't miss one episode.

I lit a cigarette with nothing but my t-shirt and panties on. I couldn't believe that I had allowed myself to smoke cigarettes. I had quit, and here I was again, back on Newports because of the stress I was experiencing with the so-called love of my life. There were knocks on my door; I got out of bed and went to see who it was. Seeing him through that peephole resurrected some feelings I didn't know were there for a minute. I didn't know why he had come over. He had been playing with my feelings for years, so to see him on my doorstep at this time of night just made me feel wonder what the fuck he did to Legacy for her to put his ass out. He sure wasn't here because of free will; there had to be a damn reason.

"Why the fuck are you really here?" I turned around and asked him in the middle of the darkened bedroom. I had finally let him in after he banged on my door a few times. When he entered my house, he locked the damn door, like his ass was at home, and walked straight to my bedroom without my permission.

He smelled like Polo cologne and Dove soap. Why did he have to smell so damn good? That smell made me weak each and every time;

that was part of the reason why he got in my door, even though I pondered on the other side about leaving him out there.

"Look, bend that ass over, and shut up for a minute," he said as he roughly turned me around and pulled my panties off my ass. I could tell by his slurred words that he was drunk as hell. Besides, who didn't like a drink or two on a Friday night? He stroked my body endlessly; the dick was so fucking good to me. It was fat and long. No matter how long we had been fucking, it was like each time we fucked, he dug another hole in me that I didn't know was there. The pleasure didn't last long, not past ten minutes, and I was so disappointed. I remembered when he used to make love to me all night long. Now, all he had to offer me was a quick fuck. My mamma always told me that, what a nigga wouldn't do with you, he was doing with another woman, so I couldn't help to think about how he could have been fucking Legacy better than he was fucking me!

"I'm going to ask you this question again; Sydney, why are you here and be honest? Don't change the fucking subject like you did before you bent me over and fucked me for a measly ass ten minutes!" I turned on the light after hopping up out of my bed to find my underwear and put them back on.

"Measly ass ten minutes, huh? That was the best ten minutes you ever had in your got damn life. You will never find another nigga to fuck you the way I do; that's why you're threatening a nigga with his child, just so I can come and put all nine-inches up in you. When I was fucking you, I was your daddy, so respect me and stop asking questions!" This was the same ole' Sydney, always saying some slick ass shit and thinking he was about to continue to lay up in my bed.

"Why the fuck are you here? You don't love me; you love her, right? So, tell me why you ended up at my doorstep and not home with her right now on this good ole' Friday night?" I could tell that my attitude had done it. All I wanted was answers, but this nigga was looking at me like a bitch from the streets was speaking to him, not the woman he had known for ten years. For ten years, this nigga had wasted my got damn time! I taught this nigga everything - how to lick a pussy, how to stroke a pussy - and this was how he treated me! He showed off with the next bitches, showing them what the fuck I had taught him!

"You know why I'm here. Why can't you just chill and let shit flow sometimes?" He grew angry, got up, picked up his clothes, and started to place them on his body. Each moment with him was questionable, and I never knew how long my time with him would last before he went back to her. A part of me told me to enjoy the time I had and not say anything, but then there was that part that I always listened to. I always ended up regretting it right after he walked out of that door when I laid in my bed and woke up alone.

"You always find a reason to leave me; you don't love me anymore?" I whimpered, secretly wanting him to feel sorry for the things he had done. I wanted him to make it right and wanted him to stay so that we could be a family again.

"I love you for the sake of our daughter; I love you as my baby's mother. Nothing more, nothing less. I gotta go," he said before he walked out of that door. Each time that he left felt like he was walking out of my life all over again.

As the days grew older, I grew colder and numb. Many times, I contemplated suicide, but each and every time I did, my kids walked in the front door with my mother, coming from daycare and school.

I had given my whole life to this man, and it had gotten to a point where I didn't feel like there was shit else to give to someone. When you give your all to someone and they throw that shit away, like it didn't mean a damn thing to you, it makes love a little more nonexistent, and you really don't want to try again. No matter how bad I wanted to get my shit together, I couldn't. I had decided that since he wanted that bitch, I was going on a rampage. There was nothing he could do to stop it this time. I had to stay strong if I wanted my man back, and I felt like this was my last option.

I couldn't believe that Serenity was willing to help me with everything. We tried to dig up as much dirt as we could on Legacy, and it all had to start with a background check. Sitting on that computer, about to pull up her information, I had the biggest smirk on my face. Trying to find dirt on her made me feel better. It felt better than a tall glass of Cîroc, with freshly sliced pineapples, going down my throat.

"Damn, another dead end. Seems like this bitch is made of angel dust or something. We can never find shit on her. She is perfect; she doesn't do shit at all. Look, why don't you just leave this girl alone? Why do you keep putting yourself through this shit, Tisha? I am the definition of a rider, and you have always known that. We have been close since we were little girls, but with that being said, I cannot sit around and watch you do this to yourself!" Serenity flipped on me; she turned her face the other way, so she wouldn't have to look at me. She was tired of me, and I knew that.

"If you don't want to be around while I'm doing the shit I feel I need to do in order to get my family back together, then there is the door. I am not making you stay here!" I got up from the computer desk and slammed the laptop down, almost breaking it.

"Are you mad at me for speaking the truth or mad at that girl because you can't find shit on her? I don't know. I don't know that girl from a can of paint, but have you ever considered that he may have found the girl he feels like he needs, while you're sitting around waiting on him to come back to a home he isn't coming back to? There is a good man out there, plenty of them, but you will never find him because all you do is push men away and chase after a nigga! That shit ain't appealing, and it definitely isn't healthy one bit. You're going to kill yourself being wrapped up in a man that isn't wrapped up in you, and you're too young to end up in a casket! You hear me, Tisha? I am not burying my best friend; I refuse to carry your casket! What about them babies? Will your mother continue to look after them while you entertain yourself with these shenanigans?" She grabbed my shoulders and shook me, like she was trying to shake me back into reality.

"I'm fine, and if that's how you feel, that's fine. But like I said, you can leave. I can do my dirt by myself! Fuck a rider, especially if this is what a so-called rider does. If you wanna complain about riding, then you're riding in the wrong mothafucking car! I've parked, so you get the fuck out!" I walked over to my door angrily and opened it, creating a way out for her.

"Bye then; call me when you come to your senses!" she yelled, and then she walked out of my house, and I slammed the door.

I had become deeply depressed, taking anti-depressants, and wasn't my normal self. The more time passed, the more my kids ended up at my mother's house. Life was like a blur, a cloudy blur, and I had yet to find my way out. No matter where I went, which route I took, it always seemed to be the wrong one. My so-called friends and associates always came back to me with rumors about Sydney, and that never made anything better. I had heard so many things throughout the weeks - that he was engaged to Legacy and that he had babies here and there that he wasn't claiming. Hell, one day while in the grocery store, I bumped into a girl who had a daughter, and her daughter looked identical to Rihanna. On many occasions, I could have presented the shit that I heard to Legacy, but then I thought, what would I do if I were her? I would have accused the next bitch of lying, so I kept my mouth closed. She had it coming, one way or another, and it was a matter of time before she was hurt, feeling like she wanted to die, like I did.

Chapter 17: Always Two Steps Ahead

Legacy

Sitting on my couch and eating chocolate covered cashews, while watching CSI Miami, always put me where I needed to be. It was relaxing and often took my mind off many things that were going on. I was into my show hard when I got a phone call from my friend, Shamirra. She said that her baby's daddy's cousin, Kathy, told her that Tisha's bitch ass was trying to go deeper, asking people about my got damn background so that she'd have some type of dirt to break me and Sydney up. I had also heard that she had been on Google, paying for background checks and shit, and nothing came up. See, that was the reason I stayed completely to my got damn self because, obviously, she had a fucking weak link in her circle, dishing out all of her dirt. Although I hated taking information from third parties, I always found that the resources were handy. I tried so hard to block this bitch out, but her attempts were bothering me to the fullest.

Sydney walked into the room, and all I felt was hostility. Looking at his face, I couldn't help but feel like he was the reason behind all this nonsense. I went into the bedroom, attempting to ignore him, but he followed me, trying to put his hands around my waist.

"Get the fuck off me, Sydney!" I yelled, yanking his arms from my belly and waist, and then, I turned around to let his ass know I meant business.

"What the hell is wrong with you?" he asked with a smirk on his face, trying to play the confused card.

"You know what the fuck is wrong with me, Sydney. Listen, I have always loved your daughter like she was my own, but at the end of the day, this fucking nonsense with Tisha has to end. I can't keep dealing with this, and I am starting to believe that you are still fucking around with the bitch!" I was furious about the shit that was taking place, and I didn't know how to deal with it.

"Why don't you give her a call and ask her for you got damn self then?" he asked, attempting to appear as if he hadn't done shit at all. I couldn't believe he played the dumb role with me, especially since he knew I always found out what I wanted to know. Women could be some of the best investigators when we truly wanted to be.

"If I called her, I bet she'd say she was still fucking you. Even if she wasn't, she would tell me that she was because she doesn't want to see us together. You need to tighten up and get your shit together because good things don't last always. One minute, I will be here, dealing with your bullshit; the next, I will be packed and gone before your ass gets home from them streets. The streets don't give a fuck about you, and as far as I'm concerned, Tisha only wants you because someone else has you! When will you niggas open your eyes and realize you have a good thing?" I stared at him, looking all nonchalant and shit.

"I know what I have is good, but at the end of the day, I can't stop Tisha from doing what she wants to do, and you know that. She's mad because I come home to you every night... mad because she can't have me the way she wants. Mad because she can't get this good ass dick. Hell, she's really upset because she knows my lips are on that pussy right there every night. I love you, and you know it's hard for a nigga from the streets to show the kind of shit you ask for a nigga to show, but I try my hardest. I'm out here hustling and shit, making sure you don't have to work a day in your life; isn't that what you want?" He got up off the bed, walked slowly to me, and kissed me tenderly on my lips. All I ever wanted to see was his potential. Ladies, you couldn't tell me that as women, we don't fall in love with what we know these men can grow into. Yes, my heart was steadily beating in my chest, but even with those beats, it was clear to see my heart didn't belong to me; it belonged to him. He was my first love, my life, and all I had to do was play my position and continue to stay two steps ahead of his dumb ass baby mama, Tisha. We had it all together; life couldn't have been sweeter.

The streets had gotten more complicated for Skrilla over the months; he suspected someone was trying to snitch on him. He was moving big weight, and he suspected it was someone who was hating on him, but I knew better than that shit. I tried so hard to put him up on game, especially since I had a different thought process.

"Why the fuck do I feel like the fucking police are watching me?" he asked as we were leaving our house to hit up the mall.

"Probably because they are. You know those bitches, who you used to fuck with, are some haters because you left them alone. Shit, I wouldn't put shit past Tisha; she's probably on some she can't have you, so nobody else can type of shit. What you need to do is move differently. You can't bring that shit in this house, and don't ride around with that shit. Bury that shit in the backyard or some shit, I will plant some flowers around it, and we will lay low for a while. We have more than enough of money to survive, pay all the bills, and live comfortably." I gave him the advice he needed, not wanted, as he stared into my eyes as if I was the best thing that had ever happened to him.

"Damn, baby. What the fuck would I do without you? You are my rider no doubt." He hugged me tightly, and then we made our way to Red Lobster to get some seafood. Surprisingly, before we went out to eat he did everything I said. He hid the dope outside of the house and a lot of the money too. I deposited half of the money into a SunTrust account and the other half into a Wells Fargo account, so it wouldn't look suspicious. Our checking accounts were ridiculous, but our savings... Man, we were set for a very long time. He also purchased a safe to keep money in the house and buried some of the money. Guess that was his safe move in case I left and took all of the money I had deposited because it was only in my name, just in case.

You lived this life when you loved a thug. You didn't really ever feel safe. Each moment was as if you were living on the edge, and you never knew which day would be your last. You enjoyed expensive things, but you never caught a break because you were always looking over your shoulders. You had to watch your own back because, in this game, each soul was out for self. You had so many jealous ass people around you; yes, around you because your friends secretly became your enemies. On the streets of Charlotte, niggas were gunned down by niggas they grew up with; some of them happened to be longtime friends and family members. It was fucked up, but it was the real shit that went down that made you develop trust issues.

We were sitting there at Red Lobster, and I felt like that was the best time to lay the news that I had on Sydney. I had known this new information for the past few days, and I definitely couldn't hold back what I had learned at my recent checkup with my physician.

"Baby, I have something important to tell you," I said as I watched him dive into his crab leg and shrimp platter, which happened to be my favorite as well.

"What's wrong? Don't tell me we done came all this way, you done ordered, and now you don't wanna eat here. Shit, I know you're picky and shit, but this shit is way too good to leave and go somewhere else." He laughed in a joking manner, showing off his nice, white, bright teeth. His smile had always been everything to me.

"You know I had a doctor's appointment a few days ago," I said, trying to finish my sentence, but my cellphone rang.

"Baby, who is that?" He asked, instantly forgetting that I was about to tell him something important.

"I don't know; it's from an unfamiliar number. Sure hope it isn't Tisha; I'd hate to have to leave my meal to whoop her ass again." I smiled and then answered the phone.

"Hey, baby," he said. I didn't have to wonder who it was on the other line. I could recognize the sound of him breathing. It was my daddy, Yankee. Out of all the things I could have said, I should have asked him why he left me like that. I could have asked why he had chosen the streets and put the streets before his children. The only thing that I could think to ask was, "How'd you get my number?"

And so he replied, "It wasn't hard to find you. Your mother gave it to me."

I couldn't believe her. She was always so damn forgiving when it came to him. If it was me, she could hold a fucking grudge about me leaving a fucking soda out on the counter for it to go flat after it had been opened, but not him. With him, it was much different. He left us out to rot; the decisions he made had a major impact on our lives. It changed my mother, and she made some fucked up decisions. She had been a horrible parent to me; I lost my daughter, London, because I didn't have a stable support system. I had so many reasons why I was angry with him, but when I took one look at Skrilla, I realized I was dating a man that was just like him. If I could love Skrilla for who he was and what he did, then I had no choice but to forgive my father for the mistakes he made. Otherwise, I would have appeared to be a hypocrite for not giving him a chance when I was fucking a nigga who did the same shit my father did.

"Wow. She is a piece of work. I wasn't expecting you to call me, and furthermore, whose number is this? This isn't a number from the prison. I know nobody snuck and gave you a cellphone, Dad. You can get in trouble for that." I hurried up and jumped to conclusions, erasing out the one possibility that was a reality.

"I wanted to surprise you, baby girl. I got out today. Your daddy is free," he answered as I sat there in awe, about to lose my appetite.?

"That's great, Dad, but can you call me later? I'm about to eat, and I'm really hungry." I made up an excuse to get off of the phone, but I could tell that he was so happy just to hear my voice that he agreed, told me he loved me, and let me go.

"Who was that baby?" Skrilla asked, almost finished with his food, although I hadn't touched any of mine.

"That was my father; he is out, but I would rather talk about it at home," I suggested.

"Hey, waitress. Bring my wife a to-go plate for her food please, and we will take some of those good ass cheddar biscuits to go as well," he said, handling the situation since he could tell I wasn't feeling it at all. My father, Yankee, had never been there for me; shit, I hadn't gotten any phone calls, not even letters, unless my mother hid them or some shit. All those years I needed him didn't matter if he was locked up behind bars. He was still my daddy, I was still his baby girl, and he wasn't there. Although I found all the reasons in the back of my mind why I should have given him a fair chance, I wasn't great on rebuilding relationships, so I knew it would be hard to speak to him until I was completely ready. I couldn't see him until I was ready to offer him a fair shot at starting all over, starting fresh.

We packed up my food and the biscuits that my greedy ass nigga ordered and then headed home. On the way home, I felt like someone was following us, and I could tell that Sydney did too because every turn we made, they made as well. He pulled out his .38 from the glove compartment, and I placed my hand upon my forehead because I knew what time it was. My nigga was far from a punk. He didn't run and hide from anybody, and he wasn't going to start today. It was all dark out, so he could barely see, but as soon as we pulled over, he got out and told me to stay in the car.

"Nah, fuck all that. I'm coming with you," I stated as I got out, ready for whatever. I was dressed like I was ready with jeans, a pink, Polo shirt, and some white and pink Jordan's. My hair was brushed neatly into a ponytail with Jam. I was beautiful, but whoever this was following us had me fucked all the way up.

He held his .38 and stood in front of me. I could tell he was upset that I didn't listen and sit in the car. At the end of the day, bullets didn't have names on them, and his BMW wasn't fucking bulletproof.

The driver's door opened, and Skrilla pointed his gun towards that direction. I shook my fucking head once I realized that it was Tisha.

"What the fuck are you following me for? I was about to kill your fucking ass!" Skrilla yelled as Tisha came closer. I took off my earrings and prepared to beat this bitch's ass again because this was the last straw.

"I followed you because you didn't answer your phone. Our daughter needs shoes and clothes, and you're too busy lounging with your bitch!" Tisha said with rage, although she knew to keep her distance from me.

"I will be a bitch, just for you, bitch. Keep me out of that shit; I ain't got shit to do with why you almost got killed for following us around town. Stop using his daughter as a pawn, bitch. He does everything for her." My fist became tight and ready for her mouth.

"I will handle this shit, baby," Skrilla said as I stepped from behind him to stand beside him.

"Look, I do everything for my daughter; you don't have to stalk me for a damn thing. We were busy; that's why I didn't answer. I would have called your ass back. Shit, you act like she doesn't have clothes on her back and shoes on her feet right now. She has all of that because of her daddy. When was the last time you bought shit for her? All you do is make sure those bills are straight and look to me for every fucking thing else. She needs clothes, but you're walking around rocking five hundred dollar purses." He reached in the car to put his gun away while he talked to his baby mama.

"Yeah, the only reason she rocks Michael Kors is to try and compete with me, but hey, we can all see who's winning." I laughed and waited for her to do something. Surprisingly, she didn't try to do a damn thing. She just finished talking shit, like always, speculating on what she thought in her own mind.

"How in the hell do you sleep at night, allowing another woman to talk to the mother of your child that way? She treats me like shit in front of you, and you let her. It's like you like that shit. She doesn't have any kids by you; she is a fucking side piece turned main chick!" She screamed out in anger. I could tell that if she didn't have so much pride, she would have cried. Surely, that was against the code, and she had broken it before. Never cry in front of the next chick because that was not a good look. That was a weak ass move, and that was something for the next chick to discuss with her friends and laugh about.

"Little do you know, bitch! I am the baby mama too. I have the latest ties with him, and we are happy. Unlike you, we have a life, and things to do, so carry on, bitch. Kiss Rhianna for me and goodnight," I rubbed my belly and smiled. What was supposed to be a private moment for my man and I was used as a vindictive move, and although I should have been ashamed of the way I used my pregnancy at that moment, I was tired of this bitch and wanted her to know that she needed to stay in her got damn lane. We got in the car and left. Thank goodness she got the picture, and she went her own separate way because the look on Skrilla's face showed I had more than enough explaining to do.

"When were you going to tell me you were carrying my seed?" He glanced at me for a second, taking his eyes off the road to see if I felt bad at all for displaying my pregnancy in such a way.

"I was going to tell you when we were eating dinner tonight, but my father called. Then, I was going to tell you at home, but babe, when she tried to throw shade and insinuate that we didn't have ties together, I couldn't help myself. I wanted her to know that I share a special part of you as well, babe, and I hope you aren't mad at me for that part."

"We will talk about it later. Shit, it's been a hell of a night, and I know you wanna eat and watch a movie. I bet I better not catch you with another cigarette in your mouth though after tonight," he stated, worrying about his unborn child and the decisions I had made with my body. I had smoked cigarettes for the longest; hell, the menthol calmed me down a lot. I knew I needed to quit, and if I didn't have the perfect reason before, I did now.

We pulled up at our house, went in, and I ate my crab legs and shrimp with some good melted butter and lemon pepper. He didn't bring up my father or the pregnancy, and I was at peace with that for the time being, although he did throw my pack of Newport's away right in front of me. I couldn't argue with him though because that was what good men are supposed to do. We peacefully slept the night away, until the morning came. All we heard was banging on the door. I rolled over, wiped my eyes, and jumped up out of the bed, but not as quickly as Skrilla did.

He went to the door, as I stood in the doorway of the room, and all I saw were police officers standing in the doorway.

"Excuse me. Can I help Y'all?" he asked, furious as to why they were at our door, waking us up, at seven o'clock in the morning.

"We have a warrant," they said as they grabbed his arms through the doorway and handcuffed him. We knew off the gate that it was some stupid shit because they didn't try to search the house. It was as if it was behind someone else or something.

"Call my lawyer," he yelled at me before the officers took him outside. I started crying. I tried to be strong for him, but I couldn't hold back the tears. I mean, when you were with a hustler, you always had the fear of your man being arrested in the back of your mind, but that reality doesn't sink in until it actually happens.

I dried my tears and called his lawyer, just like he asked me to do. I didn't know the code to the safe, so I headed to the bank to withdraw a few stacks, so I could be prepared to pay any fee I had to make sure my baby would get out.

Yankee called me while I was out and about, trying to handle business, and I ignored his call a few times. He probably thought I was ignoring him when, truth be told, he had really bad timing. Like I said before, I had to make time for him when I was truly ready to give him a fair chance.

It didn't take much to figure out that Tisha had something to do with this shit. I called the jail and asked why he was being held, and they told me for simple assault. I knew it, but I couldn't believe she would go as far to lie on the father of her daughter because she had gotten the memo that I was his child's mother to be. She had made it seem like he hit her, maybe beat her ass, but at the end of the day, he wouldn't do no shit like that because he knew better, and he was with me the whole night.

It was a pretty tough wake up call for me, all because my dude had to sit up in jail overnight, and that was one of the loneliest nights I had ever experienced. Yes, they were plenty of nights when he stayed out late, but he always came home, so this was different. I couldn't sleep at all. The more the hours passed, the more afraid I grew of sleeping there alone, knowing he was locked up. His lawyer worked wonders though. He was out the next morning because the officers who arrested him never read him his rights, and with the help of his lawyer, we were able to prove that he was at home with me. It was just a completely different situation that wasn't called for, and I hoped he wouldn't actually put his hands on that girl because, picking him up the next morning, I could tell he was more than pissed off.

"I can't believe this bitch would go this far. Her ass needed to be locked up for lying and shit like that. Now, that's fucked up, man. I could kill this bitch!" he shouted and teared up. It was rare when you saw a thug cry, but shit, believe me, the tears were there. They had feelings too.

"We can get through this together; you can't go killing anybody because I need you. I don't know what I would do without you; this shit isn't sitting right with me right now. Shit, I wanna whoop her ass myself!" I kissed him and let him know I was on his side. It just seemed as if he wasn't the same person; I should have expected that because being behind bars for some bullshit can take a toll on you.

Shit went downhill from there. He went from being caring to always angry. I could tell he was taking his problems out on me because of what Tisha had done to him. My nights became cold as hell, and the hours he would come in at night became later and later.

Like any other woman, I got upset. I went from being upset to being angry. I went from angry to furious, and well, from furious to being completely fed up. I started making plans for myself and stopped being stupid. I wasn't going to allow him to cheat on me and do me dirty. I wasn't going to keep allowing him to come home at any hour of the night when I knew for sure that there was always some other nigga out there who wanted his spot. I started doing me, and there was no better feeling.

I packed up a few bags of my things, grabbed all my small belongings, hopped in my car, and drove away from the house. I had decided I wasn't coming back until I knew completely that he had gotten his shit together.

It hadn't been a good thirty minutes since I had left, and no matter how bad I wanted to answer his calls when he realized I was gone, I knew I couldn't.

"Baby, I love you; I know you left. Please come back," he texted, but I just erased the message and kept it moving. I was halfway to Atlanta, and I was definitely about to be turn up for as long as I wanted to.

As soon as I got to Atlanta, my pregnancy hormones grew stronger, and all I wanted to do was eat.

I pulled over at Wing Stop Stand, and as I got out, I couldn't believe who I was bumping into with his sexy, brown-skinned ass. He was a piece of work, and just looking at him showed me that black definitely didn't crack.

"Hey, stranger. Sow are you doing?" he asked, staring me up and down. I didn't know exactly what to say to him; he looked good. Vonne had been like my first love, the first guy I felt comfortable with, and I didn't have a clue as to how much I missed feeling safe until that moment right there. He had neat, freshly done dreads, no more corn rolls, and he was clean from head to toe.

It was only a matter of time before I came face-to-face with him to deal with these unresolved feelings we had developed back then for one another. The circumstances of our relationship and the outcome seemed to be merely out of our control.

"Hey, stranger; how are you?" I asked, nervous, as my palms were damn near sweating. I was standing there like a woman who had forgotten how sexy she was, a woman who had forgotten she had all the juice. Men looked at me everywhere I went, and although I had gotten knocked up, I still hadn't lost my hourglass figure. I still had my beautiful, butter pecan brown-skin complexion; I never had acne or anything that could compromise the length of my beauty.

"I'm doing good; it's good seeing you. I'm hungry right now; I've been waiting for these wings and fries for going on ten minutes," he replied, I could tell he was nervous as well. I could also tell he was hurt; it was like he was trying to avoid eye contact with me. I guessed he didn't want to look into the soul of the woman who had stolen his heart and ripped it into pieces.

"Well, it's going to take a while; that lets you know they're fresh. You definitely don't want to eat something that's precooked, just sitting out there to come in contact with God knows what." I took a deep breath, preparing myself for what was next to come. I walked over closer to him and tapped him on the shoulder, attempting to share a friendly gesture. I just wanted for him to forgive me and for us to have some kind of friendship left after everything that had taken place.

"Yeah, you're probably right. Anyway, what brings you to Atlanta? I thought you still lived in Charlotte?" he asked. I could tell he was trying to instantly read me from the inside out. He finally had given in to avoiding my eyes, and I didn't blame him. I was always told that by looking into the right set of eyes, you could get lost. It was like losing yourself in someone else, and I was sure that was what he had done.

"I needed a vacation; you know Atlanta is my second home," I added as his eyes searched deep inside of mine, almost as if he was looking straight through me. I could see that glare once again, the glare that he once had for me back then. It was like I could see the feelings he once had for me, all by looking into his face, and although they were suppressed, they had never left.

"That's good. My number is still the same in case you get bored. For real, don't be afraid to hit me up, so I can spend some time with you later. We have a lot of catching up to do." He tried to find an excuse to hurry out of there as soon as his food as ready. I knew it was ironic for us to meet again that way. It had been two years since I had been with him; time had gone by so quickly. Two years had passed since him and I dated, and I could look into his eyes and tell those years that passed by may have been comforting for me, but it had been a rocky rollercoaster ride for him.

I nodded as he paid for his food and left. I loved the thought of spending time with him, but catching up was something I surely didn't want to do. I didn't want to sob to him about my relationship with Skrilla; it would break his heart and make me feel weak.

I ordered my food, waited, paid for it, and then left.

135

I arrived at the Marriott and paid for a hotel room. Shit, I end up paying so much money for a full week that it made me feel like I should invest in a place for myself here in Atlanta. I made myself comfortable and turned on the television as I kicked off my shoes and got ready to eat my wings and fries, with blue cheese on the side for dipping.

I decided to call Vonne after an hour of watching some boring T.V. show. After all, I had to do something to keep from answering Skrilla's phone calls.

"Hey, I was wondering if you would like to come over?" I asked, patiently waiting for an answer. As I listened to him breathing over the phone, it reminded me of the times when we were together. I would just lay on his chest and listen to him breath while his heart beat in my ears.

"Yes, I will be on the way in a few. Text me the address to where you are," he said, right before hanging up the phone. He sounded excited, yet I was still nervous as ever. I texted him the address to the hotel and the room number. I jumped up to freshen up because I didn't want to smell like wings and blue cheese when he arrived.

I washed my body, stepped out the shower, and dried off. I sprayed my favorite fragrance, *Nude* by Rihanna, on my body, and then I put on some shorts with a tank top. I had come a very long way from the girl who used to wear the *Sex On the Beach* body oil from the beauty supply store.

I placed my ankle socks on my feet, put some Mac lip gloss and eyeliner on, and then proceeded to the bed to wait for him to arrive. It didn't take long for him to get to my room, and I opened the door for him. The first thing I thought was that he smelled so good, and I was such a fool for a man who wore the right fragrances.

"Hey, you got here pretty quick." I examined his body language with one quick look, right before locking the hotel room door behind him.

"Well, you're not too far from where I stay. I stay in Decatur still, but I'm no longer living with my mother. I finally got my own place, but

I still help my mother with her bills and help make sure she is well taken care of. Besides, I'm all she's got." He sat on the bed, and I admired his Air Forces. They were cute. I was sure he wore them because he couldn't afford to buy Jordan's. That was alright though because he was living right, trying to make an honest living.

"You have always been a good man, Vonne; I don't expect that to change any time soon. So, let's get to the point. Who is the special lady in your life right now?" I asked, trying to find out if he had moved on like I did.

"There isn't a special lady in my life, Legacy. The only girl I ever loved was and will always be you. I couldn't have you, so I decided not to settle for less. I don't think there will ever be another you," he stated as he placed his hand on my lap.

"That's sweet, and I want to let you know that it is truly my pleasure to share your company right now." I smiled, although there were some things that were eating me up alive now.

"What do you have there in that bag?" I asked, wondering what he had brought with him. Vonne had always been so thoughtful. It may not have cost a lot of money, but he always took his time out to buy me some kind of gift.

"Well, you allowed me to be in the presence of a queen tonight. What queen doesn't like a drink every once in a while? Especially since you're on vacation." He pulled out a bottle of pineapple Cîroc. He knew that was my favorite; he always knew what to do. For a second, it almost slipped my mind that I was pregnant, and I almost indulged in the vodka.

"That's very thoughtful of you, but I can't drink anything right now," I said, placing the bottle that he had just handed me down on the nightstand.

"That's not like you to pass up a drink. You still smoke, don't you?" He looked puzzled, trying to read me like a book. He grabbed the bottle from the dresser, poured himself some in one of the plastic cups he had bought, and took a sip while waiting on my response.

"Nope, I don't do any of that anymore. I'm sorry," I said, looking into his eyes. I could tell he was about to ask me the question I wanted deeply to avoid. It wasn't that I was embarrassed about my pregnancy, but I knew that if I told him, he would want to know who was the lucky guy.

"Why are you not drinking or smoking, shawty? You pregnant or something?" he asked, looking into my eyes with a look that screamed please say no.

I paused for a minute, trying to find the words. I knew I was about to hurt him again, but I would rather hurt him with the truth than with lies. I didn't like lying, and I hated people who did. That was never a wanted trait for me period.

"Yes, I am pregnant. I just found out not too long ago, so I'm not sure as to how far along I am. I am still a little uneasy about the situation. I am taking a break from my unborn child's father, and besides, I'm starting to feel afraid because I've been having more dreams about London. I still can't get that last day that I saw her out of my head. She was crying for me, and I couldn't do a damn thing about it. I can't help but feel like I am an awful mother, and I don't deserve another shot at motherhood because I didn't get London back. I failed her, and I am only going to fail this child as well. My baby's father is a drug dealer, living the street life, and there's a possibility my child may end up like me - a lost individual with no direction and a father doing Fed time." I cried my eyes out, listening to myself speak on everything I had been through, and what I was going through really impacted me in the worst way at that moment.

"Shawty, first of all, you will be a damn good mother. God doesn't make any mistakes; you will get London back, and you will be good at this thing called life. You walk and the ground gets jealous; you breathe and the air starts hating. You are unique, and I need you to see that. As far as the nigga you're seeing, I know exactly who he is. It's the nigga you left me for; it doesn't take a genius to figure out he is a drug dealer though. Hell, you rock the best clothes, you carry Marc Jacobs purses, and that shit's not cheap. But Shawty, when will you realize that a Marc Jacobs bag ain't gonna make you happy? That shit is temporary, just like your man's lifestyle. You need someone in your life who isn't afraid to live for you. Someone who will do the right thing so you won't ever have to worry about him being behind bars." He placed his hands on my face, and although I was hurt at the moment, he helped the pain go away.

I didn't know what to say, so I just listened, and we chilled. We spent the night watching corny horror films and sharing intimacy. He didn't try me, and that was big because I needed that, a man who showed me that I was beautiful but also displayed that it wasn't always about being physical.

We woke up in the morning. I passed out in his arms after a long night of chilling and laughing about any and everything. We went to Waffle House around eight a.m. to get something to eat.

"I will have the all-star breakfast please," I ordered, and he ordered the same.

We sat and ate until we were full and couldn't eat anymore.

"Look, Legacy, I'm not trying to take you away from your man. All I'm saying is that you deserve to be safe and so does your baby. You deserve a man who comes home to you every night from work - not one that comes to you fresh off the block. I love you, and I will love any child you have - even if they don't belong to me. Just remember that." He kissed me slightly on my cheek and took me back to my room, only for us to say our goodbyes. Vonne was and would always be a good man, but I didn't know if that was enough. I didn't know if the love I had for either one of those men was enough to make me choose either one of them. If Sydney was the man for me, then why hadn't he gotten his shit together by now? Two years had gone by and time waited on no man.

Furthermore, if Vonne was the one for me, why didn't it work out in the first place? And if he wasn't the one, why did we keep crossing paths? There were so many answers that I needed, and I had to just allow these questions to ponder in my mind. That was the problem. I always made quick decisions to hop in the next nigga's bed, and that shit had to stop. There was one thing that was certain; the pregnancy made me sleepy because, after eating those waffles, I crashed and was out for a long time.

After being sleep for some hours, I awoke to some horrible abdominal pain. It hurt like hell for me to sit up, but as I did, I could tell something was terribly wrong. I pushed the blankets off my body and noticed a puddle of blood on the white sheets. I quickly picked up the phone and dialed 911 so that I could get some help. Once the paramedics arrived, I was transported to Grady Memorial, only to find out that I had had a miscarriage. Instantly, I felt like this was all punishment because I was stressing myself and had left home. It was too much on my body, too much on the baby. I asked the doctor to call my aunt because I was in no shape to drive myself home; at least that was what they told me.

Once my Aunt Calina got to the hospital, after her four-hour drive, I knew I'd have a lot of explaining to do. She greeted me, squeezing me tightly, while trying to put all the pieces together.

"How did you have a miscarriage, and when were you going to tell me you were pregnant? You are so secretive; it doesn't make any sense." She shook her head, and as I opened my mouth to tell her what happened, I just knew she'd say, 'I told you so.'

"I just found out, but I came here alone because I needed to get away from Sydney, Auntie. He has been cutting up lately, and I just couldn't deal with that. I'm just ready to go home," I explained.

"Well, why isn't he here? And how are you going to get your car home?" she asked me. I wondered the same thing. He should have been here by my side; instead, he was upset with me, so no matter how much I called, he didn't answer. Here I was, alone, up until my aunt came to my rescue.

"Those are pretty good questions. I will figure it out, but I do need you to take me back to the room to get my things. I guess I will call Vonne and see if he can come and pick up my car and park it at his house for the time being."

Calina took me to the hotel, and I gathered my things to hit the road. Vonne had one of his friends drive him there, so he could pick up my car.

"Hey, Vonne. Thanks for coming." I limped to pick up my suitcase, still feeling pretty weak in my legs, and my stomach was cramping so badly.

"It's not a problem at all, anything for you," he said, reaching for my suitcase so that I didn't have to carry it to the car. My aunt had a glare in her eyes, and I could tell what she was thinking. She smiled the whole walk to the car, watched him put the suitcase in her trunk, and then, we watched him drive off in my car as we pulled off as well.

"That boy loves you very much. I'm not the smartest person in the world, but I will say this baby, you have some tough decisions to make. I know that Sydney loves you too; I remember the way he used to look at you when he picked up from my house, but at the same time, is that something you want? A man who loves you but doesn't know how to come in contact with his sensitive side to be there for you in serious times of need. On the other hand, Vonne is all that and more; he probably just can't offer you as much when it comes to materialistic things," she said as we drove to get on the highway to make our way back to Charlotte.

"Seems like everyone knows what I need, except for me. I know I have decisions to make, but right now, Sydney is on thin ice and I'd like to keep Vonne in the friend zone because I don't want to play with anybody's heart. I just don't know if I am what he needs right at this moment," I answered as I laid my head further back onto the seat and made myself comfortable so that I could fall asleep. I drifted into a deep sleep, and when I woke up, I couldn't believe I had slept that long. We were just arriving in Charlotte, and I couldn't wait to get back home to find out why Sydney hadn't been there for me. I know I didn't pick up the phone for him when left, but I had a damn good reason. I was just hoping his reason was going to be truthful, and I hoped deep down inside that it wasn't over between us yet. We pulled up at my house, and I got out. I jumped out of the car, leaving my luggage in the trunk, trying to tell my man what happened to me. I opened the door and entered the house.

"Baby," I called out, but he didn't answer. I knew he was home because his car was in the driveway. It was in the middle of the day, and he loved to take naps, just like I did, so assuming he was sleeping in our bed, that was where I went looking for him. I couldn't believe my eyes as I opened up the bedroom door. His baby mama, Tisha, and he were laid up in my got damn bed. I picked up the fucking vase and threw that shit at the both of them; it hit the wall, missing their heads by a few inches. They jumped up out of the bed, and I stole off in Tisha's shit. This bitch had some nerve to feel comfortable enough to come and lay up in my shit. I whooped her motherfucking ass all around that got damn house, and my aunt came in right when I was about to hop off in Sydney's shit.

"Niece, no! Please stop. They are not worth it." My auntie tried to grab me and calm me down the best way she knew how.

"They've got me fucked up! This nigga had all of me; this bitch put him through the most bullshit, and here they are, laying up together in my got damn bed. The same bed that I picked out my got damn self and had delivered along with all the other shit I picked out for this fucking house!" I teared up and then grabbed my stomach as Tisha stood there, looking stupid. She picked up her wig from off the floor and tried to put that shit back on.

"I rock virgin Malaysian hair, bitch. Get you some," I smirked, just knowing I had gotten the best of this bitch.

"You really need to chill out; you just lost your baby. You shouldn't be doing all this. You can end up back in the hospital." Calina picked up my purse off the floor and stared at Sydney, waiting for an explanation.

"You lost our baby?" Sydney looked sad. With a disappointed, blank stare, he tried to come a little closer, almost forgetting his baby mama, Tisha, was there.

"You still love her? After all you told me last night, I can see it in your eyes," Tisha said, tearing up.

"This ain't about you right now, Tisha! Legacy, when and how? I'm sorry, baby," he said, trying to grab my arm.

"I will send for someone to get my shit. Y'all can have each other. Tisha, you wanted my spot, bitch? Well, you have it. I hope you can handle the job qualifications because this nigga is a bit too fucking much!" I walked out with my aunt, her arm in mine, trying to comfort me.

"It's going to be okay, baby. We're going to my house. You know you always have a room in my home, no matter what." We got into her car and drove off. He didn't know who he was fucking with; after all, I had that nigga's money. I would never do anything to hurt him, wouldn't call the police on that nigga like his own baby's mother did, but like I said before, niggas don't know when they have a good thing until it is far gone and not going to come back.

My aunt was there for me, helping me heal along the way, always giving me comforting words. She even started taking me to church. Vonne was such a gentleman that he brought my car home and took a greyhound back to Atlanta. I cried on his lap before he left, and he reassured me that I would get through it. I thought this was the end of things, but little did I know, the worst was yet to come.

I sent my Uncle Jay to pick my things up for me from the house that I once shared with Skrilla, and my uncle told me that it took everything in him not to whoop that nigga's ass.

Two years had gone down the drain in my eyes, and all I had was a broken heart, a whole lot of money in the bank, and a fucking trip to the health department.

Why did he do this to me? Was Tisha fully satisfied with her tactics to break us up? I didn't know, but one thing was for sure, I was coming out on top, despite everything I had been through. You should never try to fix some shit that wasn't broken, and if it was broken, you should check the damage before you try and repair. Some damage was so bad that you just had to throw the shit away and buy something new. You would miss something that had value to it, but a knock off was always disposable. That was where I was at this point in my life. Sydney and I were broken as a whole, and I just didn't know if the damage that was there was worth trying to fix. I was so tired of holding onto shit that didn't benefit me in the way that it should, all because I felt it had sentimental value. I had been through hell and back. I stepped over crack pipes in my own fucking home because my mother couldn't stop doing crack. She was a well put together crack head; nobody knew but me. Maybe I was like her in so many ways, cleaning up a fucked up situation to make it look pretty. Shit had to change.

Chapter 18: Deceit at Its Finest

Tisha

It was June 5th when I got up out of bed, fixed myself some breakfast, showered, cleaned up, and got dressed for work, when I realized I wasn't getting any younger. I went to sleep twenty-nine years old and woke up thirty-years old. I had to work on my birthday at BB&T, and the love of my life still hadn't left the younger, fresh meat he had left me for. I had spent so many months trying to find some information on this girl, but no matter what I did, nothing came up. Still, I was unaware of how I would use the information when I found it because Sydney was full of flaws and was willing to accept a woman who wasn't perfect either. Look at me; hell, I was full of flaws. I was a dark skinned bombshell; at least, that was what other people told me, but there were days when I woke up, feeling ugly.

I headed to the office after eating a piece of toast with two scrambled eggs and sat at my desk as usual. I started feeling a little sleepy, so I left my desk for a brief moment to fix myself some coffee, and I overheard a conversation I wasn't ready for. A conversation I didn't expect to hear at all.

Curtis Brown was a loan officer at my job, and the coffee machine was close to his office. I overheard him talking on the phone about an important adoption case, one where he had gained a daughter named London. I also heard they had to change London's last name to try to stop her birth mother from finding her. As a mother, that made me feel horrible. I couldn't imagine losing my children, but when I heard the last name Hayes, it all came together. I had always known that Legacy had a daughter, but it didn't come to me until I heard the last name. Sydney mentioned London before when I argued with him about having

Rihanna around someone who didn't know how to be a parent because she didn't have any kids; that was when he felt the need to tell me about London. I didn't know the exact situation. Although I heard some things here and there, I just always knew that London was never with Legacy.

That wasn't the information I was looking for, but it was something. I grabbed my coffee with extra sugar and cream, realizing I had put way too much cream by being nosy, went back to my desk, and worked hard like any other day.

I was happy to get off work that day, and I was confident that I would cause havoc. I didn't tell a soul about the fresh news I had discovered. I kept it to myself and waited on the right moment. I had been trying to call Sydney, but he had made it clear that he didn't want to talk to me unless it was about Rihanna. I was hurt; I knew he was in love with this girl because I even tried making him jealous by dating another man, and that didn't work at all. He told me he was happy that I was finally happy and that we needed to continue to be co-parents to our child. I was crushed, and if things couldn't have gotten any worse, I followed him and his bitch. Hell, I was right outside of Red Lobster, watching them eat all good and shit, and when they suddenly left, I decided to follow. My baby daddy pulled over, tried to shoot me, and then that bitch had the audacity to tell me that she was pregnant. I had him arrested out of spite. So what? Nobody was fucking perfect, but at least I could admit to my faults.

A few weeks had gone by, and he called me over to his crib because he wanted to see Rihanna. He wanted to see his daughter, and I wanted him. I hadn't had him in a while. He was actually trying to do right by Legacy, but fuck all that because he never tried to do right by me.

"Where is my daughter?" he asked as he opened the door for me. I looked around, peeping out the scenery, and the house was completely empty.

"Where is wifey? She isn't here, huh?" I strutted my way to the couch and made myself comfortable.

"Look, I called you because I wanted to spend some time with my daughter, not because I wanted you coming over my house by yourself, questioning me and shit. If Legacy comes home, what will she think?" he stared at me, pulling up his pants, and tightening his belt, I guess so I wouldn't think I was getting what I knew I was.

"I could care less what the fuck Legacy thinks. Matter-of-fact, you and her better be a little nicer to me and give me what the fuck I want before I fuck up her world." I got up and moved in closer to Sydney, unbuttoning my jeans, becoming horny as hell.

"There's nothing you can do to hurt my baby; she is strong as hell. Stop fucking with us, alright? Get the hell out my house and come back with my daughter. That's what the fuck you can do!" he yelled at me, and that was when I felt like I had no choice but to play the only card I had left.

"I can hurt her so fucking bad that she would turn away from you and never look back." I smiled, although I could tell he still wasn't buying it.

"I'm going to use my bathroom; by the time I get back, you better be gone." He left the living room, and I quickly went over to the counter where there was a glass of Cîroc. I knew he didn't waste liquor, so I reached in my purse and put some codeine in it. I knew it would make him pass out. He'd be out for a while, and I could do whatever I wanted to him after that. I searched around for his spare key, found it right on the entertainment system, and placed it in my purse. He then walked out of the bathroom, looked at me, and said, "Damn, you ain't gone yet?"

I shook my head and left. I parked up the street from his house, to give him at least forty-five minutes for the codeine to work, and then I left the car across the street, walked over to the house, and let myself in.

I undressed myself and got into the bed with him, hoping that when he woke up, he'd see me naked and would instantly want me the way he used to. I was not sure how I ended up passing out with him, but I didn't even get any dick at all. I woke up to Legacy hitting me, screaming and shit. This bitch had some nerve putting her hands on me, and if she knew what I knew, she would stop while she was ahead because I was going to make her sorry. I didn't give a fuck what the cost was; this shit was bigger than Sydney was. I had a point to prove - that I was not to be fucked with.

As soon as her and her raggedy ass aunt left, Sydney was staring me down, I could tell he wanted to lay hands on me; instead, he turned around and headed to the door like he was going to go after her.

"I wouldn't do that if I were you. You know how Legacy's daughter, London, was taken away? Well, I know a way to make sure she never sees her daughter ever again. I know the adoptive parents, and I can make sure they know she is dating a big time drug dealer. That's not a good environment to raise a child around; now it it?" I threw it all out there, and damn, it felt good as fuck.

"Now, that's some stupid ass shit. I don't want you, and I never will. Think about what the fuck you're saying though. I am Rihanna's father as well. What if that was you with your dumb ass?" He walked away, leaving his own house. I was standing there replaying what he said to me before he left, the way he starred me up and down. He hated me with a passion; he probably wished he never met me, and for that, I didn't want to live anymore.

I waited for him to come back, and he didn't. I grew depressed, and if that wasn't enough, I had taken the codeine back out of my purse. I sat there staring at the bottle of prescription medicine, contemplating on taking my life. I slowly opened the medicine, removing the cap, and then I started to drink. As soon as I drank a little, my cellphone rang, and when I picked it up, I saw my mother calling. It wasn't the fact that she was calling that stopped me from taking my own life; it was more so that the picture I had taken with my mothers and children at the park was the picture that popped up on my phone each time she called. I took that as a sign, answered my phone, and then headed to my mother's house to see my children.

I had to do something differently, at least try for my babies. I decided to move out of Charlotte and get my shit together, at least for the babies.

I went to my mother with my pain and my new idea. Although she didn't want me moving to another state, she supported me one hundred percent.

"Baby, you have to do what's best for you. Don't depend on any man to make you happy; you have these babies to live for, and they need you more than anybody." My mother kissed my forehead and gave me a hug.

"You are right, Mama, but I love him so much. I've invested so much time on him, Mom." I cried my eyes out, searching for some confirmation that I was right to feel the way I felt, but I was dealing with my mother, and she always kept it real.

"Yes, you love him, and he may still love you baby, but at the end of the day, love isn't enough, and you don't deserve that thing he is giving that he calls love. A man needs to learn how to love himself before he can love someone else; he needs to learn to be secure with himself before he can be secure with just one woman. If he hasn't put a ring on your finger by now, he may just be running from commitment, and that other girl better watch her back, fucking with my baby, because I don't play about mine. Take them babies home,] get some rest, and call me if you need me." She helped me gather my children's things, and I left.

I spent weeks trying to find a place, something affordable with enough space to accommodate the kids and me. I started looking in Myrtle Beach, South Carolina, and was able to find a nice place about ten minutes away from Ocean Boulevard. I got a job at Fuddruckers, and although working at a burger joint wasn't ideal, it was something to help pay the bills until I could get a reference to get another teller job at a local bank. I never thought I could allow a man break me down so low to the point that I didn't know who I was anymore. I loved that nigga more than I loved my damn self, and that wasn't good at all. I made a choice to start all over, to take a chance, and try to find myself. I needed to find Tisha and learn to put Tisha first before I ended up dead or in jail behind a nigga who I rode for but who wasn't even willing to walk for me.

It had been a month since I had last spoken to Sydney. It wasn't like he hadn't called; he did every day. I'd give the phone directly to his daughter and put him on speaker so I could hear everything he said. When he attempted to get information out of our daughter, by asking where we were, I'd grab the phone and hang up on him.

I didn't need him coming down here looking for us; I needed my space. My hair had started growing back, long and healthy, after years of wearing wigs because my hair had been breaking off because of the stress that I had placed upon myself. I had started taking some responsibility, and although I hadn't fully grown, I was making progress, taking one day at a time, and that was all that mattered. My nails were pretty and long, my face was clearing up, and I had put on an extra ten pounds in all of the right places. There was a guy who I worked with that held my attention more and more as the weeks went by. I even felt comfortable with bringing him around the children. He had been through a rocky relationship like I had, he was working, making his own money, and in his spare time, he taught volleyball on the beach to groups of children. His name was Deon, and he asked me on our first date three months after I caught his interest and he caught mine. I could tell the connection we shared was more than physical; it was intellectual, and that meant a lot.

"Your phone is ringing a lot, beautiful. You're not going to answer that?" he asked as we enjoyed our lunch break together over two bacon burgers and some fries, with a fruit punch on the side.

"No, it's not important. It can wait because I am having lunch with you." I giggled, feeling like a girl in high school, on a date with her first crush.

"Well, tonight, I'm taking you on a real date. We are going to a buffet; you and the children need to be ready by seven." He smiled at me and reached over the table to hold my hand.

"That's so sweet of you. We will be ready by six thirty, just for you." I reached over the table and planted a kiss on his face. We finally got off break and went back to work to finish our shift and get off early to enjoy some fun time together.

I picked my kids up from school and daycare when I got off of work. We went home, I got them dressed, and then got myself dressed. We were ready by six thirty, like I promised. He picked us up and took us to a buffet where there was plenty of everything, especially my favorite, crab legs and shrimp of all flavors and kind. We all ate very good, shared some laughs, and by the time we were finished, he paid for the dinner. It was one hundred dollars for him to feed us at that buffet, so I knew he had it bad for me.

I couldn't wait until the date was over so I could go home, give my kids a bath, put them in bed, call my mom, and brag about my new guy.

My house was clean, smelling just like Febreeze, and was quiet with the kids sound asleep, so I finally fixed myself a glass of wine and called my mother.

"Mom, I have some news to tell you," I said as soon as she answered, and I heard her voice on the other line.

"Baby, you need to hurry and get back here. Sydney has been in a bad accident. He hit a deer and ran off the road; he needs you and his child right now. You need to come, bring the kids to me, and head to Carolina Medical Center.

"I'm coming, Mom," I sniffled. Tears rolled down my eyes, and disbelief arose in my mind.

I instantly hung up the phone, packed a few bags, placed my kids in the car, and started driving to Charlotte North Carolina.

I was stressed out, trying not to wreck doing seventy miles per hour all the way there. I kept thinking that this was my time to prove to him that I would be there for him in ways Legacy couldn't, my time to show him I loved him, and that I would always stick by him. The fact that I even had a boyfriend was instantly wiped out of my mind, and just like that, I was addicted to Sydney all over again. It was eleven o'clock when I left; thank God, my children slept the whole ride, which took three hours and forty-eight minutes. I had finally arrived in Charlotte and had to slow my speed down. At that time of the night, police were everywhere, just looking for a reason to pull people over and give them a ticket. I pulled up at my mother's house, and her living room lights were on. She had waited up for me. I could only imagine how she felt because, no matter what Sydney did to me, no matter what transpired between us, she was still like a mother figure to him.

I took my children in and dropped them off. Looking at the clock, I couldn't believe it was 3:00 A.M. I went straight to Carolina Medical Center. When I got there, I couldn't believe my eyes; I was at a loss for words. I was right back at square one.

Chapter 19: A Thug in Love

Skrilla

Pow. Pow. Pow. Shots rang out inside of one of my favorite nightclubs on Independence Boulevard while I was sitting in the damn car, listening to some J. Cole. I couldn't believe these niggas were shooting at my niggas. I hung around a few hot heads now and then, but I didn't find out they were hot heads until I was stuck in the middle of some dumb shit. I took my gun out and started shooting back at them niggas when they ran up out of the club. One of them niggas hit the ground when he fell, and that was all she wrote. I cranked up my car pulled off, and went home to hide my fucking gun. Shit hadn't been the same since Legacy left. It was bad enough that she left, but shit got worse. I didn't give a damn about anything anymore. If a nigga wasn't reckless before, I was damn sure living on the edge now.

"Damn, nigga, you need to slow your roll. A nigga doesn't need to end up back up in jail and shit. That's why I don't like going nowhere with y'all hothead ass niggas!" I put my nigga, Rio, in check. This nigga was always doing some dumb shit. Shooting at niggas at the club was the last thing a nigga needed, but at the end of the day, I would always ride for mine and expected the same in return. It was a code in these streets, and we lived by loyalty.

"Nigga, that wasn't me. Eric got into a fucking fight with some lame ass niggas. The niggas pulled out their tools and started blasting at us first." He pulled out a blunt and was about to light that shit up.

"Nah, nigga. Put that shit up and get the fuck out. You're my nigga and all, but after that hothead nigga shit, you can't chill here. I gotta get some rest anyway. A nigga's got a long night ahead." I pushed the nigga to the door. I couldn't believe this nigga showed up at my house anyway. Anybody could have been following him, and I didn't need that shit.

"Damn, nigga; I will go. I had some bitches I needed to fuck good tonight anyway," he bragged. Then, he lit his blunt anyway and smoked on his way out.

I shut my door, locked that shit, took a damn shower, and got ready for bed. *'Damn,'* was all I could think; her pictures were everywhere. I had fucked up in a major way. I allowed my woman to lose my baby while I was getting my relationship fucked up by my own baby mama. I should have listened to her, but I never did. All those bitches I fucked and those long nights in the trap wasn't worth losing her. All I could do was hope that it wasn't too late for a nigga.

All I ever wanted was a down bitch, one that didn't complain. A female that would hide my drugs, help count this money with me, and I could ball out on.

Legacy had always been that and more for a nigga. She was the type of woman who went shopping for herself and brought you back some shit, too. That type that would hide dope in her pussy when you were about to be pulled over by the cops. She was a dope boy's dream.

That wasn't a nigga's only problem though. I kept calling Tisha to see my daughter, and this bitch wouldn't even answer the fucking phone. I even went by her house and realized she had moved out, so I panicked. My life was fucked up, and I didn't know how to fix anything. I always fucked up everybody's life who was affiliated with me - at least that's what it seemed like.

I had been by Legacy's house a few fucking times, and she wouldn't come to the door. This time was different because, although her aunt gave me a smug look, she still let me in.

"Why haven't you answered my calls and my texts? Shit, I've been by here so many times, and you still won't talk to me. Is there another nigga or something?" I asked her as I stood there in the middle of her aunt's living room. She was sitting on the couch with her sexy, brown-skinned ass, makeup all done up, hair looking fly, but she had on some pajamas and a t-shirt. That shit was sexy as fuck to me. She wasn't afraid to be herself. She didn't feel the need to dress up all the damn time, and it looked like she was wearing a nigga's t-shirt.

"What's the real reason why you came tonight? You want your money back? Huh?" she asked me. It was like she was taking me for a fucking joke.

"Fuck that money! I lost my soon-to-be wife, okay? I want you and only you." I got on my knee and pulled out the engagement ring I had bought her. I hoped she accepted because I couldn't stand rejection. Plus, I had never done something like that for nobody else. As long as I was with Tisha, I had never proposed to her.

"That's a beautiful ring and all, but is this Sydney or Skrilla I'm talking to? You know you Gemini's have split personalities; I never know who I'm dealing with because, the last time I checked, you had your bitch ass baby mama up in our bed. Oh, and please don't try and tell me you didn't fuck her because that's the main lame ass line you niggas try and throw at a bitch!" She got up off of the couch. I could tell from all the hostility that she was extremely upset. What was a nigga to say when she was ready to disregard the truth from the beginning? I had been drawn in by Tisha so many times and fell for the bullshit. However, that day I wasn't. The one moment I didn't do some vile shit, I was paying for it anyways.

"Look, baby. You already made it clear that if I told you the truth, you wouldn't believe me anyways, so what am I supposed to say?" I got up off my knees, still holding the 18-carat, yellow gold, diamond ring that cost me fifteen thousand dollars.

"I hear you, but I need actions not words. And no matter what you tell me right now, I'm not going back to that house that I caught you in with your baby mama. It's going to take a lot more to get me this time.

The problem is, I gave it up a little too fast. The first fucking night? I was out of my got damn mind! What the fuck was I thinking, giving you all of me that quickly?" She cried until her eyeliner started smearing on her face, and I walked over to hold her. I pulled her hand out and placed the ring on her finger because, no matter what, I only wanted her. I knew for a fact that if I lost everything tomorrow, she'd be the type to be there regardless, holding me down through the tough times. Hell, I couldn't say the same about my baby mama.

I took her into her bedroom and shut the door. Hell, her aunt was already sound asleep. I pulled down her pajama pants, ate the pussy, and sucked all the juices out until she fell sound asleep too. I laid there with her, watching her while she slept, just thinking about the steps that I could take to fix this shit. I knew I was in there with her. Now, I had to find my conniving ass baby mama.

I got up and left. I texted Tisha's mama and told her that I needed to talk to her. Hell, I was willing to do whatever I had to do in order to be in my daughter's life - even if I had to take child support out on my damn self so that I could get visitation. It was dark as hell, and I was speeding. It seemed like I had a heavy foot because every time I got behind the wheel, I couldn't help but go fifty or more miles per hour.

That shit happened so fast. I had a cup of Cîroc and lit up a blunt to vibe while I was driving. It seemed like I was in the country. I was going on so many curves, trying to get to Tisha's mom's house. I took a sip of Cîroc, and the next thing I knew, a fucking deer came out of nowhere. I hit that shit and blacked out. That was all she wrote.

I saw my life flash before my eyes. A nigga was sitting in the BMW, all unconscious and shit. I saw my childhood with my mom and dad, happily married and together. I saw my half brother, who passed away when I was a teenager. For a minute, I thought I was dead - until I woke up in a cold ass hospital room, all banged up. I couldn't say shit. I had tubes all down my throat, and I was in so much pain and didn't know what was going on. When I tried to lift my hands, I couldn't. There was no feeling in my legs. I didn't understand. I heard the nurses talking about my surgery and about my arm being broken. I heard them talk about the injuries to my spine. I kept thinking a nigga was going to end up in a fucking wheelchair, crippled for the rest of my life. I started thinking about Legacy and how I wanted her by my side. I didn't think of anyone besides her, my daughter, and my mom. They say when you were on your death bed, you think about the people that mattered the most. Well, I guessed it was time for me to stop fucking with Tisha for good because it was clear that if I had to choose between the two, I'd choose Legacy without a doubt.

Chapter 20: Standing by A Thug

Legacy

It had been a few months since I had been staying with my Aunt Calina. It wasn't easy leaving Skrilla, so I wouldn't front. I cried for the first week, each night when I laid in my bed to go to sleep, but then, I asked myself what the fuck was I crying for when I wasn't the one who had done wrong. He blew up my phone and showed up at my house, but I just couldn't fall for that shit again. I had to get my life back where it was supposed to be.

"Baby, hand me those spaghetti noodles," my aunt said as she prepared some ground beef on the stove. She knew spaghetti had always been one of my favorites, and she was always willing to do whatever it took to cheer me up.

"Here you go, auntie, and can you please fix that four cheese garlic bread? I don't want plain garlic bread tonight," I suggested as I pulled the bread out of the deep freezer.

"I was thinking the exact same thing," she agreed as I fixed a cup of Amsterdam Vodka.

"I know this is something you may not want to talk about, but have you considered paying for a lawyer to get London back?" From the way she looked at me, I could tell she was as hurt as I was about the situation and wanted a resolution.

"I will have to hire a lawyer after I find my own place and get a stable job. I'm thinking about going to school to become a certified nursing assistant; I've always wanted to work at a hospital. I just have to get my shit together all the way around, you know?" I sat at the dining room table and grew quiet because I started thinking hard. She was right, and I had the right concept of things as well. I decided that, first thing in the morning, I would start looking into going back to school because that was the first step.

I had cut all ties with Vonne because I decided that it wasn't cool to play around with his heart. I wasn't the one for him. We weren't meant for one another, so I had to give him room to fully move on and find someone who was right for him. I still had my heart wrapped up in Sydney. My love for any man I was with had always been strong, and it would always take a lot to fuck that up. I guess that was how I knew he was the love of my life. I had never dealt with this much shit with a man and still kept going back. I was a female player back then, always getting free shit from men; I had a little black book and all. Vonne fucked up one time, and that was it for us - but Sydney was another story.

After my aunt and I finished eating, there were a few knocks on the door. We both looked out the window together and realized it was Sydney.

"What do you want me to do?" she asked with a frown on her face, ready to curse his ass out.

"You can let him in. I guess it wouldn't hurt to see what he has to say." I flopped down on the couch and waited for her to open the door for him. He was happy as hell getting in; he hadn't even had the door opened for him in months, heard my voice, or any of that. I couldn't believe he proposed to me, but I think that was what made me break down. I couldn't help myself. This was the moment I had waited for, and I had gone through a lot of shit just to get this man where I wanted him. I had to let him know words didn't mean shit. Actions spoke louder, and he had a lot of proving to do before I did anything. Most of all, I made it clear that I wasn't moving back in with him anytime soon, and I was never sleeping in that fucking bed ever again.

I knew he would tell me he didn't fuck Tisha, but who knows? I didn't trust either one of their asses.

The way he ate my pussy as I cried made every inch of my body tremble. The sexiest part of it all was that he didn't try to fuck at all. He ate my pussy, sucking every bit of pussy juice from the inside of my walls, until I passed out.

The same night, I kept getting phone calls. That's when I looked over and realized that Sydney was not by my side. I looked in my call log and realized I had twenty-two missed calls from a number I didn't recognize. I finally called the number back to see who was it and why the fuck they were blowing my phone up, but it was a voice I didn't recognize.

"Who is this?" I yawned, waiting for the unknown person to reveal who they were.

"This is Malcom, Sydney's cousin," he said. I could hear the sense of urgency in his voice, but I had to cut him off anyway.

"How did you get my number, and why are you calling me so many damn times at this time of night?" I asked as I got up and made my way to get something to drink. I was thirsty as hell.

"Sydney was in a bad car accident. Legacy, he needs you right now. We're at Carolina Medical Center." That was all he needed to say. I rushed to my room, grabbed some jeans, Ugg boots, and a sweater, and slipped them on.

I jumped in my car and made my way to the hospital. It felt like the longest drive ever. When I arrived, that was the most anticipated feeling I had ever felt. I didn't know if he was okay or what was going on. I greeted his friends and family in the waiting room and had to break the news to everybody so they wouldn't be in the blue.

"Hey, everyone. I can't believe this is happening. He just left my house. I woke up, and he was gone." I broke down in tears because I couldn't hold it in anymore. His mother gave me a hug to console me and told me it would be okay. When she let go of me, she looked down at my hand, and I could tell she was admiring the rock on my finger.

"You and Sydney didn't get married, did you?" She looked worried, trying to find out if I was her daughter-in-law yet.

"No, he proposed to me tonight." I held out my hand so that everyone else could see.

"He must really love you. I knew you were the one for him the moment I met you. I knew you were different," Malcom said, and it made me feel good to hear that. I just couldn't bring myself to explain any of the things that we had been going through. It definitely wasn't the time nor place. Besides, they probably knew anyway because Sydney always kept a close-knit relationship with his family and friends.

After I took a seat, his mother sat down beside me as we waited patiently for the doctor to come out and tell us the news. He was in surgery. I was told he had broken his arm and injured his spine. My hands were trembling, and it started pouring outside. I stood up and went to the window to look at the rain shower. It always soothed me in the best way, bringing comfort to my soul. I turned around, and there she was - Tisha. In the back of my mind, I had a feeling she would show up, but I just didn't know it would be that soon.

"What the hell is she doing here?" she asked, looking around at Sydney's family, searching for some kind of answer.

"You need to chill out with all of that, Tisha. My son is in surgery right now. We don't need this drama up in here." Sydney's mother made her point, trying to calm Tisha down. I stood there quietly, trying to be a lady.

"Fuck all that, he isn't even with her. They broke up months ago, so why is she here?" she asked again. I could tell they were trying their best not to hurt her feelings, but I guessed she was asking for it.

"Sydney would want that girl here. I know that for a fact, Tisha. You really need to chill out and stay in your lane," Malcom added, staring her up and down as he attempted to save her from a world of embarrassment.

"He wouldn't want that bitch here. She ain't shit," she added, flipping her hair back over her ears and face like she was about that life.

"He would want her here. That girl you're calling a bitch is his soon-to-be wife; they're engaged," his mother explained. The look on Tisha's face turned very sour as she looked at my hand, searching for a ring. Once she spotted the ring, she started crying, as if she was in the worst physical pain ever, and she almost went on a rant.

"Fuck that bitch, and fuck Y'all two-faced asses. Always in my got damn face and shit; Y'all fake as hell." She looked at everyone while expressing her feelings. She was obviously hurt and still carried deep feelings for Sydney.

"We aren't fake, and at the end of the day, we all need to be cordial for the sake of Rihanna," Sydney's mother added as she stood up and stared Tisha down. Tisha had balled her fist up as if she wanted to fight. She then turned around and walked out of the waiting area. We assumed she had just left the hospital all together.

The doctor finally came out and told us he had a good recovery. He was stable, the surgery had gone well, and we could go and see him. His mother went in first, and then, I was up next. When I entered the room, I could tell he was in pain.

"Hey, baby; I shouldn't have left you tonight," he said, trying his best to talk. I didn't want him explaining anything.

"Baby, please don't say anything. You need to relax and just enjoy my presence, love. The most important part is that you're okay. I'm not going anywhere." I sat down on the bed right beside him, kissed him on his cheeks, and then went to sit in the chair available in his room.

I stayed by his side, just like a real woman should, and watched him get well enough to leave the hospital.

I had the bed removed from the house and had a better king sized bed put in. That way, I didn't have to worry about sleeping in a bed he may have fucked other bitches in.

I was amazed as to how quickly Sydney healed. For having a metal plate in his arm, he sure moved it around as if it was never broke. The process was rough at first; he could barely walk on his own. I had to help bathe him, prepare all of his meals, and clean the house each day. I had to make sure all of the bills were paid, but hey, it was nothing. Small things to a giant.

When he was capable of doing all those things on his own, I could tell from the look in his eyes that he had a newfound respect for me. I could tell he cherished me a lot more than he did before. It took him four months to heal enough to where he could do everything on his own and didn't have to rely on me. He was upset because he had been missing out on money; our bills weren't exactly cheap. We paid twelve hundred dollars to live in our house, but the cost was worth not living in the hood anymore. Including the money we spent all together on bills, we weren't broke, but he was running out of the money that he kept in the house. A nigga who hustled almost never felt comfortable asking his woman for money.

"Baby, can you please cook for me? I think I want some shrimp and rice tonight. I will be home a little late, but don't wait up on me. I've got to make some moves." He put on his clothes and got ready to leave.

"Okay, I love you." I kissed him and allowed him to leave in peace. Things had gotten so much better with us. I could see a big change in him, and I knew I didn't have to worry about him sleeping around with other women. However, I could tell something wasn't right when he left. He said he was going to make some moves, but he left his cellphone behind - the phone that all the junkies called him on. I rushed out the door to give him the phone, but it was too late; he had pulled off. I never had a problem with Malcom, but Sydney was spending a whole lot of time with him lately. That was odd because, the last time I had checked, Malcom had just welcomed a new baby boy into the world with his longtime girlfriend, Ivey, and had stopped selling drugs for good.

I prepared dinner, sat down, and watched the news. It was odd how there was a string of robberies happening in different areas around town, and no suspects had been caught either. But hey, that was the typical day in Charlotte.

I had been feeling a little weird lately. I hadn't seen a period in three weeks, so I was definitely nervous. I had gotten a pregnancy test at the drug store, but it had been days since I hid it in the cabinet of my bathroom. I was procrastinating because I was afraid of the results. I knew I wasn't ready to be a mother, especially after the talk I had with my Aunt Calina about getting London back. I wanted my little girl to be there when I brought another child into this world. Until then, I had to be focused. On day three, I finally decided to end the procrastination and take the test. I sat on the toilet, panties pulled down to my knees, just waiting on those results.

"Fuck, fuck, fuck!" I repeated as I let the tears flow down my face. At that point, I had made up my mind not to tell Sydney and keep it to myself. I couldn't let him know because I didn't know if I was ready for that. More than anything, I was ready for him to stop hustling, but I just didn't know if he would do that. This man had been a hustler before me, and he had always been a product of his environment. He loved nice shit and felt like that was the only way to get it. Now that I was pregnant, I had to make the necessary steps to get London back in my life. London was, and had always been, my priority, and that would never change. I had to get to the bottom of my case; and figure out why I was treated unfairly and why the caseworker seemed to be working with the adoptive parents. But first of all, I had to find those adoptive parents.

Chapter 21: Stick Up Kid

Malcom

"Lil' nigga, you betta have my shit by the time I get back before I fuck you up!" I got in this lil' nigga's shit, who I had running one of my corners. Lil' Ron was always fucking up. He couldn't control his niggas on the corner, and they were always coming up short. I got tired of that shit. My girl, Ivey, loved the finer things. She had a taste for Michael Kors and Marc Jacobs. She loved designer clothes, and when these lil' niggas ended up short with my money, it meant I was short with Ivey's money. She didn't play that shit.

"Man, I swear I'm gonna get these niggas right, and then I'm gonna have the rest of your money, Malcom. I just need one more week. Please!" he begged me like he knew I was going to kill his ass right then and there. Maybe it was because of the name I had made for myself in these streets.

"Nigga, you've got two fucking days, and that's the last chance you're getting with me," I warned him before I drove off in my all-black Lexus. Like I was saying before, I had earned a name for myself. Niggas knew that when I pulled up on their corner, playtime was over. I did Fed time, not because I did some fucked up shit, but all because I don't snitch. I was running work for a big ass distributer, and once the Feds started watching, they pulled any nigga off the streets that was associated with Big Tim. I had fucked up big time, but if I never ended up in prison, I would have never met Ivey. She worked at the prison as a guard, and she looked out for a nigga when I was down and out. She made sure a nigga had money and even snuck cell phones in, all for a nigga to talk on a phone that wasn't tapped.

Hell, if it wasn't for prison, I wouldn't have met my day one, either - my nigga, Sydney, aka Skrilla. We made a pact that, once we got out, we would keep in touch. Also, whoever got out first would look out for the other one, and that was exactly what happened. He got out first, became the plug, and looked out for a nigga. A lot of people didn't know that Sydney was the plug. Shit, he believed in staying low-key. He was the type of nigga that would tell your ass that you could go buy sneakers, clothes and shit, and a nice car, but to keep it simple.

He'd say buy Jordan's, but not mink coats. Buy a BMW, cop a Lexus, but don't buy a fucking Maserati. Do shit that made sense. Don't go and get all flashy because going back to prison wasn't an option.

He was smart as hell, and I learned a lot from that nigga. He looked out for me and gave me kilos of cocaine for the low. He was like my brother, and I would take a fucking bullet for him. We'd go and ball out occasionally. We were one in the same. We loved drinking Cîroc, and sometimes, we fucked some of the same bitches together. We didn't allow our women to hang out together because that shit would be a recipe for disaster. So, we kept Ivey and Legacy far apart from one another on purpose.

"Man, you won't believe this shit; these lil' niggas fucking with my mental again. Every time I turn around, they are fucking with my money. I need to give Ivey a few stacks, so she can go shopping, or she will probably leave my ass." I sat on the phone with my nigga, giving him the real and uncut as always.

"Man, your girl shops more than she cooks. Nigga, you need to pay for her to take some cooking lessons. Eating those burgers and pizzas and shit every day is unhealthy." He laughed while he talked a little shit.

"Shit, everybody can't have a Legacy. She likes material shit too, but she doesn't trip when you don't buy the shit for her. Plus, she can throw down in the kitchen and make a nigga wanna eat at your house every night." My girl, Ivey, was fine as hell. She was a redbone with short hair.

She kind of resembled Halle Berry, but his girl was the full package. Shit, if I had a girl like Legacy, I wouldn't ever fuck up. But then again, a nigga like me needed to test the waters every now and then.

"Hey, nigga, stop thinking about my woman; you're gonna make me come and put these hands on you." We wrapped shit up and then got off the phone.

A nigga had come a long way. Shit, I wasn't living on West Boulevard anymore; a nigga had a big ass house in Ballantyne. I couldn't be like Sydney in every aspect of my life. Shit, I had to make sure my crib was at least laid. I kept a few trap houses where I kept all my dope; I never wanted to keep that shit in my house. Ivey quit her job and moved down to Charlotte with me from Hickory, North Carolina, close to Marion Correctional Institute. That was where I was incarcerated and where she worked as a prison guard. I had never been to college. Since a young nigga, I was thuggin and pushing work. Like I said before, I had never been caught - that was until I linked up with the wrong connect. The Feds had been watching him for a long ass time, trying to put a case together on him. Nigga was like the new generation Scarface or some shit. Every time I went to pick up my packages, the nigga always had cocaine laying around with some bad bitches from different countries, sniffing that shit. He had pills, weed, whatever you wanted. I never went to his house and got fucked up. I always went for strictly business.

When I came home from prison, I had a hustle. If this shit I was doing wasn't working, I'd find another hustle. Shit, a nigga would hustle until his last breath, especially if he didn't wanna struggle and live by the fucking book. What the fuck was a regular job anyway? I'd rather build my own fucking empire than help the next man build his. Besides that, I hated living the kind of life that was routine. Shit, I couldn't see how people woke up and did the same shit every day, sacrificing their free time for them to end up getting a paycheck that was only enough to pay the bills. I wasn't going to act like hustling was easy; hell, like any other job, it came with cons. I've been shot in the back, been stabbed a few times in the stomach, and a nigga survived. I became ruthless after all that shit happened to me. Niggas were scared to even look my way. It wasn't nothing to grab a nigga, put his ass in a trunk, and demolish his ass. Hell, I was the type that would kill a nigga and show up at his funeral to pay my respects. I just didn't give a fuck, and there wasn't shit anyone could do that could change how I was.

When Ivey got pregnant the first time, I was about to give all that shit up and invest in a business or some shit to stay out of the game and keep myself out of trouble. When she lost my son, my first-born, shit became blank to me, and I was right back at it with my same old frame of mind. It seemed like when it rained, it poured. A week after I lost my son, my nigga, Sydney, was in a bad car accident that could have taken his life. I was there at the hospital, there for the recovery, and there when he fell off. Ivey and Legacy knew we were hustlers, but when we were hurting, they didn't know the extent. We didn't have bricks anymore, and to get where we were at before would have taken a few years of work. We had done spent so much fucking money on our houses, cars, and bills that our pockets were looking limp. We didn't want to ask our girls for shit because, at the end of the day, that was some pussy nigga shit, so when I went to him with the idea of a new hustle, he accepted.

"My nigga, the only way we can get back to how shit was before is if we start running up on niggas and taking their shit." I laid some shit out on the table, some shit that he might have felt uneasy about, but it was definitely easy money.

"Man, I have a lot to lose." He put his hand on his chin, like he was in deep thought, and looked down at the floor while we sat in his new BMW.

"Nigga, we also have a lot to fucking gain. You were my plug, my nigga, and I don't need another one. Shit, you know how hard it is to gain trust and respect for a mothafucka. At the end of the fucking day, we both need this money. Man, my girl would kill me if I had to start letting shit go. You know how these women think; they're always quoting the same bullshit ass line, 'I can do bad all by my damn self.' Man, I don't wanna hear that shit.

"I hear you, but shit, let me lay some shit out for you. One, I am not going back to fuckin prison, two, we ain't hurting nobody, three, we get the money and we go, and last but not least, don't be putting me on no bullshit ass licks." He dapped me up, and I shook my head, letting him know that we were on the same page. Then, he dropped me off at the crib, and he left. I knew he needed the money; I knew my nigga was going to be down with the shit. Hell, if I had dropped 60k on a new BMW, because my last one was totaled, I would have needed that shit too. Robbing niggas wasn't new to me. I had stuck up a few niggas here and there, and I had broken into a few houses when I was fifteen years old. I had come from a low-income household, and it killed me that my mom couldn't afford to buy a nigga Jordan's, so I thought I'd make a way for myself. My momma was struggling on housing and food stamps; she had all the government assistance a single black mother could get, and that shit still wasn't enough. She worked two fucking jobs, one at IHOP and the other at McDonalds, and I guess that was why I felt like I was allergic to doing that type of shit. I saw my mother, my queen, being fucked by the system, and that was why the system could kiss my black ass.

The first lick we did went smoothly. Shit, we hit a few people up when they were leaving the atm. Easy money, and I knew that since the first lick went good, Skrilla would want to go on more licks after that.

"Bitch, give me the mothafuckin money!" We had our face covered on our second lick, just like the first one, but we were at a local strip club this time. We hit a few strippers up when they left. Shit, we had two bags full of fucking money to split up.

We went back to my house to count up, while Ivey was upstairs sleeping, and we were happy with the outcome.

"Shit, nigga, what do you have over there so far?" Skrilla looked at my bag, questioning what a nigga was counting.

"Don't worry about what's in this bag, nigga. Count up!" I had to remind this nigga to stay the fuck out my business.

"Shit, nigga. I know you're just fucking around, so imma let you live this time," he said, cracking up. That was how we joked around. Shit, if you didn't know us from a can of paint, you'd think we were dead ass serious. You'd think we were enemies until we started laughing and dapping each other up and shit.

"Nigga, I got one hundred thousand over here," I explained, holding a stack of money up in one hand and a blunt in the other.

"Shit, I got three hundred and twenty thousand over here. Damn, man, we've been fucking with women in the wrong profession this whole damn time. Be too quick to trick off on them stripper bitches but too ashamed to wife them hoes. They are bringing in all the cheddar." Skrilla put the money all on the table and organized that shit in stacks with rubber bands.

"Don't let CIAA weekend fool you. Shit, they got that money because all these rappers and shit are in town; that's when they make bank," I explained to Skrilla. I felt like his ass didn't know any better.

"You're talking about the shit like you know firsthand. Let me find out you done wifed a stripper bitch before." Sydney chuckled a little.

"Shit, stripper bitches need love too; I wouldn't dare take one of them hoes to meet my mama though."

"Anyway, my nigga, let's wrap this shit up. I gotta make it home before wifey starts tripping. That's split down to the middle; we're taking two hundred and ten thousand a piece." Skrilla started to separate the money, and I helped.

"Alright, bet. That what's up; see you later, my nigga." I dapped him up, and then he left my crib.

Stick up boys at its finest. Shit, we were doing it. We never hit the same scenery, so it would be hard as fuck to catch us. We started investing the money that we were getting, buying bricks and flipping that shit. We were back to the old us… almost. Instead of him being my connect, I became his right hand man. A nigga felt unstoppable. Shit, I was on top of the world and couldn't nothing bring me down. Period.

A month had gone by, and life was good. My operations were moving smoothly, and Ivey was happy. I came home one night to roses and shit everywhere. There were a few Marc Jacobs watches and a nigga's favorite cologne, which happened to be by Clive Christian. In my head, I was thinking a nigga must have done something right.

"Hey, baby." She greeted me in the bedroom with some lingerie on. She always looked fine as hell, but this night was different.

"What's all this shit about? You must really love a nigga," I said, trying to find out what had make her want to do some shit she had never done for me before.

"Well, you have always been good to me, even when I complain and nag. You're always busy, working hard as hell, just to make sure I won't ever have to punch the clock. So why shouldn't I take the time out and show my man how much I appreciate him?" She switched her hips my way while R. Kelly was playing loud as hell. I knew what time it was because R. Kelly always put her in the mood. Every time we listened to that nigga, we ended up fucking all night long.

"I see you got your other gifts on the way up here. Well, there's another gift. It's right here; I need you to open it." She handed me a little blue box, and I was happy as hell to see what was inside.

I opened the box, and a nigga started to feel all kinds of mixed emotions. It was a pregnancy test, and it said positive. My baby was having a baby. This time around, all I wanted was to have a healthy child, and furthermore, I wanted to make sure my child was straight.

I didn't sleep much that night, but I watched my girl sleep peacefully. That was good enough for me. The next few days, I had put up a lick before I presented it to Skrilla. It was this big ass house, also located in Ballantyne, owned by rich, white folks. You could tell by the cars in their driveway that they weren't hurting. I grabbed my phone and called my nigga, Skrilla, to meet up with me at KFC. I jumped in the car, went to KFC, and waited for him to get there.

"Wassup, nigga? Damn, if you were hungry, you could have said so. I would have told Legacy to whip something up for us, and we could have chilled at the crib." He got into my car, sat down, and continued to joke around like always.

"Nigga, I didn't come here for a two piece and a biscuit. I came here so I can go over some shit with you. I know the last lick was supposed to be it for us, but man, I've got some shit lined up with this house." I reached for my cigarette and lit that shit to ease my mind.

"Look, I ain't going on no more licks, and I'm not about to hit up somebody's house, man. You know that shit is dangerous. People be having alarms and shit on their houses, the ones you can't even hear and shit. I told you I'm not going back to prison for nobody!" He was quick to judge, and from the tone of his voice, I could tell he wasn't trying to hear shit else I said after that.

"Man, hear me out; I need you on this one. I just found out Ivey's pregnant and shit. I need to make sure my seed is set before he or she gets here, man. Please? I can't do this shit without you. We do this lick, and we might not have to sell drugs anymore. Man, I'm telling you, this shit is legit. I already checked it out. We can cut the alarm cord because it's in the back of the house, get the cash and jewelry, and go. Matter-of-fact, you can be the driver. I will go in, get the shit, and will still split that shit in the middle." I had to let him know I was serious and that this was going to go right because my life depended on this shit. There was no way I would have let that shit go left.

"Man, I have a bad feeling about this shit, but for you, I will be there. I will drive. I'm not going in there, man, but you know I've got your back. It wouldn't make sense for both of us to go in there anyway. Someone needs to be watching the scenery and shit." He dapped me up and got out the car. I took a deep breath and let it out because I was relieved as fuck.

"Okay, man. I will see you in a few days. That's usually when they go out of town. So, like I said, it will be easy as hell." I gave my final input before driving off. I didn't think anybody knew how it felt when you looked around and it was hard to turn around because you felt like the world was on your shoulders. Everybody was depending on me, and that shit had been weighing me down for a long ass time. My momma needed bill money, my little brother and sister were in college and needed tuition, and my girl and my baby needed me to be a good father. This was the last time I was going to do some fucked up shit like this; we were all going to be straight and wouldn't have to want for shit. I was going to open up a restaurant and do shit the right way. I was going to some shit my seed would be proud of and make sure my girl wouldn't have to struggle and raise our child alone. Two days had gone by, and it was the day before the planned home invasion. I had my guns on deck, a car that couldn't be traced back to us, and my duffle bags, that were empty and ready to be filled.

Chapter 22: Losing It All

Skrilla

I really didn't feel like doing no lick, especially a home invasion. Shit was good between my girl and me. I think Tisha was finally getting the picture; she was letting me see my daughter and everything. The last thing I needed was to end up in jail. I could lose Legacy and Rihanna forever. Shit, Malcom had been my nigga for a long ass time, but he always seemed to think his problems were worse than everyone else around his ass.

"Nigga, where you at?" He blew up my phone at least twenty times the day of because he didn't think I was going to show up - or maybe he had a bad feeling like I did.

"I'm coming nigga, damn. Give me some time." I drove to his house after I grabbed my gun. I didn't plan to shoot anyone, but my mama always taught me to be prepared at all times. Hell, you didn't want to regret not being prepared when you're lying on the pavement somewhere, taking your last breath.

I pulled up at this nigga's house at around five o'clock. We gave the family time to leave the house and go on vacation. I got out of my car, parked it, and switched cars. He had some raggedy ass, broke down Nissan. I was wondering where in the hell this nigga had gotten this shit from.

"Where in the hell are we going in this shit? We're going to rob a fucking mansion, nigga. We're gonna look suspicious as hell, pulling up in that neighborhood in this shit for sure!" I thought this was a dumb ass decision all around, and I wanted to keep making sure he knew that shit too.

"Man, I wasn't about to pay for no luxurious car to go and rob a fucking house. That shit wouldn't make sense, man. That's a waste of money. I already went through a lot getting this car. Plus, it can't be traced back to us." We pulled off and headed to the house. When we arrived, I still felt like something wasn't right. I mean, there were three cars in the fucking driveway. There was no way to know if someone was home or not.

"Man, I think somebody is in there," I told Malcom, trying to warn him and hoping he'd want to back out of this shit.

"Man, ain't nobody in there. Them rich folks done caught a flight out of town. How in the hell can they ride a damn plane and drive at the same damn time? Please explain that shit to me. I need you to be the nigga that you've always been. Don't pussy out on me. I'm gonna go in, get the money and jewelry, and I'll be back out. It will take me about ten minutes, nigga, so don't leave me here. For real, man," he said, getting out of the car to grab his duffle bag and the shit he needed.

A nigga was too paranoid to listen to some music. My phone was on silent because I needed to be focused. No blunts or any of that shit. It wasn't the time or place to be getting high.

I was only out there for a few minutes when I heard some noise. I looked at the house to see what the hell was going on, and Malcom was coming out the front door. I was wondering what the hell he was doing coming out the front door when this nigga went in the back. The bag looked full, and he looked happy as hell. Then, there was a man standing right behind him. That shit happened so fast.

An older, white man with a golden robe and grey hair was there with a gun pointed to the back of his head. Malcom dropped the bag and moved his lips; it looked like he was saying go. I thought the older, white man was going to wait for the police to get there, so I started to drive away. As soon as I pulled off, I saw the man blow my man's brains out from the back of his fucking head. I took that fucking car, made sure there were no fingerprints in it, and got rid of that shit. I got my car from his house and left. There was no way I could look in his girl's eyes and tell her what the fuck happened. She might have been so pissed off at me that she would have had me put in jail. I went home to face the music. I had to look in my girl's eyes and tell her the truth. I knew that shit was gonna be all over the news, so I would rather for her to find out from me instead of anybody else. I rushed through the door, palms all sweaty and shit, calling out for her.

"Legacy! Legacy! I need you, baby; some shit just went down." I found her in the room, standing in the mirror, fixing her hair and makeup. She looked beautiful with her pink eye shadow, eyeliner, and lip-gloss on. She always kept it simple, and for her, a little was always enough.

"What's wrong, baby?" she asked. She could tell by the way I was panicking that something was terribly wrong. The T.V. in the room was on, and that shit was on Channel 9 News. I hurried and grabbed the remote to turn that shit off before she saw what I wanted to explain to her first.

"What did you do that for? What is wrong with you? You're acting strange as hell!" She started shaking because the last time I acted like this around her was when I thought a nigga I knew was trying to set me up. I came home, told her what the fuck was up and that I was going to kill them niggas, but I couldn't find them. Later on, I got the memo from the streets that those niggas had left town. That was a wakeup call for her. She acted brave, but after that, she watched her back. She never really trusted anyone; it didn't matter who I brought around. She didn't give a fuck who they were, and she looked at everyone as potential enemies - everyone except for Malcom.

"Baby, I'm in a fucked up situation. I really fucked up in a major way for real. If the police come here, I need you to tell them that I was here with you the whole time. I really need for our story to be straight. We were here, watching T.V. I did talk to Malcom, but I did not leave the house today!" I walked over to her and held her waist, but I could tell she already knew what was going on before I gave her the full details. She started crying like hell, and there was nothing I could do to console her because I was the reason she was fucked up like this.

"Why the fuck would I wanna do that? Is this shit on the news? That's why you turned the television off, huh?" She grabbed the remote and turned on the T.V. It was live; it was all over the news.

"Around 5 P.M., a man was shot and killed by the owner during a home invasion."

"This was you. This shit has Skrilla written all over it! I am so tired of this shit; I will not be here, not this time. For what? To watch you go under? No! For me to go under with you? I refuse to raise my baby in prison! Your best friend is dead, Sydney; what else will it take for you to change? Will it be a bullet in me the next time around, Sydney? I don't know, but I'll be damned if I stay around and find out. It's over between us; don't call me. No, in fact, I'm changing my number. Don't try to find me because I won't be within your reach anymore."

There was nothing I could say or do. I sat on the couch in my living room and watched her walk away. She packed all her shit, probably some of mine too, but who was I to stop her? The best thing I could have done for her was to let her go, at least for now.

The police came, asking me questions, but my mother had my back. She told them I was at her house when all of that occurred. I didn't even have to tell her to do that; a mother always knows instantly when their child needs help. I attended the funeral, and it was awful to have to sit and watch Malcom's family cry like that, his mother and his girl, his siblings. Everything was all wrong.

My hustle game wasn't the same; the streets had changed. I wasn't making a lot of money off of being a drug dealer anymore. Hell, I had to pick up a temporary job doing construction and shit. I couldn't collect my disability; I had been fighting for that shit since I had gotten into my accident. Being on the job was different. It was hard as hell, but at least I knew I wouldn't end up in jail. I just wished I had gotten my shit together before it was too late. Now, there was nothing I could do. My girl was gone, my friend was gone, I had visitation with my daughter, but I had to pay child support, and a nigga was struggling doing that. I had to move out of my house and find a cheaper apartment, paying only five hundred dollars a month. My car still belonged to me. I wasn't giving that shit up.

Months passed by, and I made it my business to reach out to Legacy. Shit, I just wanted to see how she was doing and let her know a nigga missed her. I knew she still loved me; she just wasn't hearing shit I had to say. She used to ask me when I would realize what I had, and I guess she was right. It was when I lost everything, and now, there was no turning back. I started doing some more fucked up shit, as if what I had already done wasn't enough. I said fuck my baby mama, Tisha, and started fucking around with a new bitch that would keep her mouth closed about our relationship. Her name was Monique, and she was alright. She was a redbone, five-foot six, with some grey eyes. On occasion, I would end up at her house when I was drunk and looking for a late night booty call. She wasn't the only one; she was just one of many. Like I said, it took a dozen females to satisfy my sexual appetite the way that Legacy could. When women became attached to me, I let them go and moved on to the next. It was as if my heart was gone, and I wouldn't love anybody else. Period.

I had tried to send roses to Legacy, but that didn't work. Tried to send her edible arrangements and all that, but she still didn't answer my calls. I couldn't even count on my hands how many bitches called me and told me that they were pregnant by me. I didn't want a baby by anyone else, so I refused to have anything to do with those hoes. I denied the babies every time. If it wasn't by Legacy, I wasn't claiming it.

Legacy told me it would happen; I would fuck around and be arrested over some bullshit again if I didn't change some shit around, and she was right. The bitch I was fucking with, Monique, claimed to be pregnant with twins by a nigga, and I didn't wanna hear that shit. Shortly afterwards, she started threatening me and threatened to kill the babies after they were born. She was crazy as hell.

I couldn't understand. It was like I wanted to do right so badly, but I just couldn't. I started to wonder if somebody had a death wish for a nigga or some shit. I knew one thing; I couldn't ever let Legacy find out what the fuck I had been up to. She could never know about the so-called babies a nigga was supposed to have because she wouldn't want shit to do with a nigga for sure. Deep inside, I hoped quitting the drug game would win her over.

Chapter 23: Seeing Is Believing

Legacy

After all the things that transpired with Sydney and me, I realized I had to get out - if not for me, then for my unborn child and London. I moved back in with my aunt, went back to school to take up being a medical assistant, and kept myself busy. My love for Sydney never left, but as long as he was Skrilla, it would have never worked out.

My classes were going well. I was progressing, and as the weeks went by, I realized that when you let go of what needed to be left behind, your future came. It became easy for you to adjust to whatever the future may hold for you. I was still in a rough place in my life, and that was when I met Chris. Chris attended CPCC with me. He was young, talented, and we were the same age. We said the same things at the same time. Damn, it was like we shared the same mind. We became the best of friends. I had opened up to him in a way I didn't think I could open up to a man. The way he made me feel was like a teenager who had her first crush. Chris was attending CPCC to become a lawyer; his ambition was out of this world. On the days I felt like giving up, he helped me, giving me inspiration to keep pushing on. He wasn't anything like Vonne or like Sydney; he was much different from both of them. He was dark-skinned and five-foot nine, so we were about the same height because I stood at five-foot seven. He had a smile that would light up your life, even on your worst days. And the best part of it all? He didn't have any children. I had to open up to him and explain that I was pregnant with Sydney's baby; that was after I had made the decision to keep him or her. Yes, I contemplated having an abortion, but my family didn't believe in abortions. Neither did I, so it just didn't sit right with me.

"Hey, beautiful. You wanna go to the movies with me?" he asked as he walked up to me after finishing his class.

"Yes, I would love that. I love horror movies; they are my favorite. The best part about it is that I have you to hold onto when I get afraid while watching." I flirted with him, kissing him on his cheek, and he chuckled. We hadn't gone all the way yet. That was what made him special. He was willing to get to know me and create a real bond with me before we shared our bodies with one another.

"That sounds good; I love when you squeeze me. I will pick you up at seven. Be ready, baby." He kissed me, and then left. I really liked that boy, and luckily, I wasn't the only one who felt that way. Everyone else felt like he was a good guy. People could see my glow from a mile away, and they knew it wasn't just from the baby alone.

"There you go, smiling again; you must really like him. I hoped you would because when you brought him home a few days ago, I could tell there was something different about him, something I have never seen in any of the other boys you've brought home." My Aunt Calina came over, gave me a hug, and rubbed my belly. I could smell the spaghetti, and although I knew it was a recipe for heartburn, it was still one of my favorite dishes. That aroma floating through her house didn't make it any better.

"Auntie, I am ready to eat. Gosh, I am so hungry. You know I'd rather have home cooked meals than eat any of that mess on campus. Besides, I need to be good and full, so I can get ready later for my date to the movies. You are right about him, Auntie. He is special, and I'm really feeling like he could be the one." I went into the kitchen, took a fork, and dipped into my aunt's baked spaghetti with extra cheese on top.

"Get out my food; I will fix you a plate." My aunt smacked my hand as I stared at her and rolled my eyes.

"You better enjoy me dipping in your food. I signed my new lease as soon as I was approved for my apartment today, so I won't be here much longer. I still have plenty of money saved up to cover all my costs, so all I need to do is go furniture shopping, and I'm good to go." I let her know that I was taking the necessary steps to become independent.

"That's good. Now, don't go rushing to move that boy in. You know you have a habit of moving too fast in relationships." My aunt set the table, so I could eat early, get ready, and then leave.

"Don't worry, I'm not… Well, I hope not, but you can't help how you feel when you're falling in love. I mean, he is everything I have wanted in a man, and I'm glad that I let Sydney go so that I could see what real love feels like." I chuckled. Finally, for the first time in a long time, I felt happy. I felt like I had someone who would protect me, someone who would stand up for me, someone who wasn't afraid to do the right thing to make me happy. This was the kind of man that I wanted to raise a family with, one who was secure in who he was and made sure that I was more than secure as well.

"Well, I'm about to go get some rest. I was placed back on third shift, so I have to work tonight. Oh, and don't do anything I wouldn't do." She hugged me and then went into her room. I finished eating and went to get dressed.

Almost everything I picked out showed my belly. My best bet was to wear this sleeveless black shirt with some dark blue jean capris and sandals. I couldn't help but recognize that my feet were swollen, but those were the things Chris made me feel comfortable with. I was beautiful. Hell, that was what I thought while looking into the mirror at myself, and finally, I didn't have to live my life always looking over my shoulders.

"Hey, baby."

He came to pick me up in his Chevrolet Impala. He even got out the car and opened the door for me. "Hey, baby; thanks for opening the r g

door for me. You look sexy." I greeted him. I got into his car and got ready to ride with him. He put on some Lil' Wayne because that was his favorite rapper. Mine was TI because I loved his swag.

"Well, we are here." We got out after we parked. He was a lady magnet and attracted women everywhere we went. I was jealous, so I grabbed him even closer to me whenever other girls looked at him. He didn't have a problem with me being territorial, and I think that made me feel comfortable with him. The more this man did, the more I fell in love.

Before you knew it, a few months had gone by, and we had finally passed second base. There wasn't anything we didn't want to do with one another because we were inseparable. I was getting closer and closer to my due date, and I still hadn't spoken to Sydney.

Sydney had no clue about me being pregnant; I never got the chance to tell him. So much time had gone by with me keeping the fact that he had a baby on the way away from him, amd I felt that it was unnecessary to tell him. I truly believed that was the only way I was able to actually move on with my life, ya know?

Chris made me want to be better. I knew the best future I could possibly give to my child had everything to do with what man I chose to raise him or her with.

Chris had managed to help me rebuild my relationships with my mother, Renee, and my father, Yankee. He put forth the effort to help me take the necessary steps to get London back. Boy was I glad that I went with my instincts, followed my heart, and stopped listening to what people told me to do because that was what they wanted - not what I wanted.

Never did I imagine that after the birth of my son, Jodie, my world would change. Chris and I would be in a serious relationship and in a kind of love that I had never felt before. I smiled each night and never cried. I was never sad, unless he was at work, away from me, because I missed him every minute that he was gone. All I wanted was to hold him, love him right, and feel his heart beat.

I never had to speculate about him sleeping around. I always knew that he was faithful and true. I walked proudly on his arms, just by knowing he was a one-woman man. Not too many girls had that. I lost friends because of the good man he was; women were jealous when they entered our presence and got a front row seat to see how good he was to me.

"Baby, can you get Jodie from daycare today?" I asked him, pulling my pants over my thighs to get ready for work. I was a bus driver for a middle school, and my job helped bring in enough income to save.

He was an intern at a law firm, studying different cases, trying to be successful. He also worked at a Hanes warehouse while he wasn't attending school. He always made time for us. It didn't matter if he worked twelve hours during the day; he would still pick Jodie up from daycare, take us to dinner, and go right back to work to clock in. We were his priority, and I never thought that would change.

"You know you don't have to ask me to pick up our son. When I get home, I need you to be ready. I'm taking you to your favorite place to eat today, R.J. Gator's." He smiled, and I felt pure bliss when his tongue met mine in my mouth, and then I waved bye with disappointment when he left to go to the law firm. I didn't understand how he did it all - spent time at law firm, attended law school, and worked a full time job. He had one more year, and law school was finished. Then, he would have the opportunity to work for the law firm for good.

When he got home, he took Jodie and me to R.J. Gator's as he promised. When we left the restaurant, I put Jodie to bed and walked into the bathroom to watch him wash his sexy ass body and admire his six-pack.

"Hey, baby. I've got something for you," I said before getting into the shower with him. We washed one another down and had the most incredible sex. That was almost every night because we fucked like we were rabbits. It was like I had some kind of sex addiction, and so did he. We were each other's fix on the regular. We never realized we were still in the honeymoon stage, and therefore, we thought our relationship would always be that way.

A year down the road, Jodie was about to turn one. Chris had been helping me fight, going back and forth to court, to get London back. I was only twenty-one, but my baby girl was about to turn six years old. I often wondered if she would know me if she saw me, but all I could do was be patient and fight my way through.

In the middle of my case, I had some horrible shit happen to me. I lost my fucking job as a bus driver, all because I was late for my shift. I stayed up late with Jodie because he wouldn't go to sleep, and although Chris helped me by taking shifts, I was still tired as shit. It wasn't the first time I was late. There were a few long nights I had with my son, and that was why things ended up that way.

I was still okay, but I felt like all the pressure was on Chris to do everything. He had to cover all the bills by himself, take care of Jodie, and not to mention, the money I needed for my hair, nails, and clothes. Sydney had been trying to reach me for the past six months, but I never felt the need to call him back. Now, things were different; hell, I needed help. It was great for Chris to father Jodie the way he had, but like any other woman, I started thinking about how Sydney was out there, not taking care of his child, because he didn't even know he had one.

"Look, Sydney. I need for you to meet me. I've got something to tell you." I called him up after not speaking to him for over a year and some months.

"I haven't heard from you in so long. Shit, where the fuck have you been? What is there to talk about now? Legacy, you know I have always loved you, but after all this time, shit has changed. I'm back with Tisha, trying to make shit work out with her and being the family man I should have been," he said, and although I didn't want it to bother me, it did. After all that shit we had been through, all the shit that girl had done, he chose to get back with her. He could have been with anyone else in the world, but he decided to move back instead of forward. The thought of him being with that bitch made my skin crawl, but I had a good man and didn't have time to play around with Sydney or his bitch, Tisha.

"Okay, I will come to you. Where do you live now?" he asked, trying to find out. I was pretty sure he noticed that I didn't live in Charlotte anymore since he hadn't bumped into me.

"We live in Concord," I answered, and instead of him hearing the 'Concord' part, all he heard was the 'we' part.

"Who is we? You're staying with someone else?" he asked, sounding all nosy and shit. See, men always had double standards. It was okay for them to move on, but the moment they found out that you had moved on, they acted as if they were about to die or kill somebody.

"Doesn't matter; just come see me and your son. I will text you the address, so you can meet us." I hung up the phone before he could ask me any questions. I texted him and told him to meet me at a nearby McDonald's, so he did. The whole ride there was so nerve wrecking, but looking at my son, this something I had to do. Since I had lost my job, I had nothing to do but think, and it was eating up my conscious that I was keeping his son, who looked just like him, from him. Jodie was light-skinned with curly hair, and he had his eyes, nose, and lips. That was his twin; hell, he looked more like him than Rihanna did.

We waited in the parking lot in Chris' car, waiting for Sydney. When Sydney pulled up, I could tell one thing hadn't changed; he still had his BMW. I got Jodie out of the car, and we went to sit in Sydney's car. As I sat there in the passenger seat, all Sydney could do was stare at Jodie for a moment because he was at a loss for words.

"Damn, why didn't you tell me you were pregnant? You knew you were pregnant when you left me, huh?" he asked, and he kind of looked upset. I chuckled and got ready to clash back, but in a calm way because I had changed for the sake of my baby. I didn't argue anymore, didn't get into confrontations, and that was more than I could say for a lot of these so-called mothers.

"Yes, I knew I was pregnant when I left; you were in the streets hard as hell. You were doing shit that could have jeopardized all of our futures, and I wasn't having my baby in prison. You thought about yourself, so I was left to think about Jodie by my damn self!" I explained, trying to get him to understand what I had gone through, what I had been feeling. He didn't know the half, and I was upset with him. You think you were over something until you come face-to-face with it again. All the feelings I had before came rushing back.

"I'm saying though; I have a son, so when were you going to tell me? He is what, one-year old now? Shit, I know I fucked up, but that's no reason to keep a man's child away from him," he said, cutting off the car completely as if we were going to be there for a while.

"He is your child, and I need your help, and that's all that matters right now." I tried to make peace the best way possible as Jodie laid his head on my chest and stared at Sydney.

"I can tell he is my son; I have strong genes, and he has my eyes, my big ass nose, and ears. He is the spitting image of me, and I'm gonna make sure I take care of my seed; I will be there for mine," he said as he pulled out three hundred dollars to give me. We sat there and talked for over an hour. He held his son and spent time with him and all. I talked to him about going back to school, having a CNA license, but persuing the bus driver position because I really wanted to work with children. I told him I was out of work but wasn't sure if I wanted to persue the CNA job because of the long hours, the mandatory overtime, and how I didn't want to miss that much time away from my son.

He told me that he had stopped selling drugs, took a temporary job, that turned permanent, and how he struggled for a while, but he was finally back to space where he was doing well again.

"I know it feels good to do shit the right way; I'm so proud of you. It took forever, but better late than never. It may take longer to get to the top by making an honest living, but hey, look at the bright side; you don't have to worry about ending up behind bars. We are all going to die someday, but I truly believe in rushing your funeral. Some decisions you make can cause you to leave this earth earlier than you are supposed to, so I'm glad things are finally looking up for you for the sake of your son." I complimented him because of his efforts and placed my hand on his, letting him know he had a friend in me if he ever needed that.

"So, what I really wanna know is, who's been loving Legacy? You already know I'm back with Tisha, but deep down inside, I'm not happy. I haven't truly been happy since you left me. I just felt like if you weren't around, there was no sense in Rihanna waking up in another home without her daddy." He looked sad as he searched my eyes for some sort of confirmation. I was sure he wanted me to tell him that I had been a single mother, maybe because he was looking for a way in, but I wasn't going to do that. I had to keep it real, so he'd know we couldn't cross those boundaries ever again.

"I have someone. His name is Chris. He has been there for me for a long time now, ever since I left and started college, he was there. I was in a rough place, you know. He was like my knight in shining armor," I explained, and I smiled, just while thinking about Chris. I could look at Sydney and tell he was miserable when those words came out of my mouth. The last thing he wanted to hear was that I was in love with another man.

"Damn, that shit hurts like hell; I thought I would be the only man you ever loved. Well, I've gotta go; I will call you again to see my son, alright?" he asked, trying to make sure it was okay for him to continue to visit.

"Okay, that's fine. See you later. Say bye, Daddy." I told Jodie to tell him bye, and he did after we got out the car. Sydney sat there, watching us walk away, watching us get into our car and drive away. I wanted him to be there for his son, but I could tell he wanted more than that.

I went back home to cook my man dinner before he came home from work. I fixed his favorite - spaghetti with pepperoni and Italian sausage. I thought about telling him that I had been to see Sydney, but when he walked through the door, I just couldn't. I felt so guilty that I had to do something to make it up to him. I had already cleaned up the house, and when he was finished eating, I put the food away. I told him to take a shower, and I freshened up with my blonde, short haircut, my face done all pretty, and my two-piece lingerie set on that was blood red. When he got out the shower, the scene was ready. I had the red lights on in the living room downstairs; we didn't need a bed because I wanted him on anything and everything I could have him on that night.

I put on Teyana Taylor and Chris Brown's song, *Do Not Disturb*, and danced all over the living room for him while he sat there on the couch, staring while only rocking his boxers. He rubbed his dick up and down as he stared at me shaking my ass and moving my body to the beat. He finally got off the couch, came closer to me, took off the two-piece I was wearing, and started kissing me from my head down to my toes. He pulled out his big dick and placed it inside of me. He filled me up so much; it made me want more all night long. We made love everywhere, on the washer and dryer, the kitchen table, and hell, even the kitchen counter. He had dinner, and I was his favorite desert. Our chemistry was still undeniable as we held each other close around 4:00 A.M. and fell asleep together, naked on the living room floor with a blanket. I had learned so much from this man; hell, it didn't take a thug to make you come multiple times, just a man who knew how to hit all the right spots.

I was his first serious relationship, and nobody wanted us together. At the end of the day, that shit didn't matter as long as we had each other.

I wakened the next morning; my love had already gotten dressed and left. That was one thing I loved about him. No matter how late he stayed up, he was still an early bird, unlike me. I cleaned up the place, got my son dressed, and opened the door as I played some music so he could chill out in his playpen. Jodie was a good baby; he always had been. He found comfort in listening to music and loved watching movies - just like his mama. I went outside and chilled with my neighbor, Dawn, who I talked to on a regular basis; I was chopping it up with her, giving her an update on Sydney and how I took Jodie to see him the day before.

"Girl, I can't believe you took that baby to see that nigga! I tell you something though, you better not let Chris find out; he will kill you. How could you do that, Legacy? You know how much he loves that baby!" She frowned at me as if I had made the worst decision of my life.

"I had to do it; you know I have too much pride to sit there and let that man take care of everything by himself. His family already looks down on me because they feel like I made him take on the responsibility of raising a child that wasn't his, and they have been distant from him. Shit, when we do go around, it's always some drama of some sort. Hell, I don't want problems in my household caused by outsiders, Dawn." It was difficult dealing with Chris' family; hell, they didn't want him starting a family with anyone until he was stable, had his job for a few years, and knew he wouldn't want for anything.

"I'm still not understanding why you had to meet up with that man, Legacy." She looked confused, trying to understand what I was trying to explain to her all along.

"I had to connect with him for financial support. I will be damned if Chris has to go to his family and ask them for anything. We go through shit just like anyone else. Just because he is the perfect guy doesn't stop us from having some fucked up problems, and it doesn't stop these bills from coming in. Do you know that I sold my Marc Jacobs and Michael Kors purses? Hell, those were the most devastating days of my life, having to give up my designer bags." I looked toward the ground and shook my head.

"Welcome to motherhood. You do what you have to do, just to make sure your children are more than good. At the end of the day, I hope you are making the right decision when it comes to Sydney because it sounds like he may have other intentions, ones you aren't aware of as of right now." She shook her head as if she was a mother and I was her child who had really disappointed her. As we were sitting on the porch, I saw a BMW drive by, and when the car turned around, I knew exactly who it was.

"Oh, hell no!" I shouted out in disbelief.

"What's wrong, honey?" she asked, trying to figure out what I was mad for.

"This nigga followed me home yesterday; he had to because that is him in that BMW, and there was no way he could have known where I stay." I got up, getting ready to go inside the house and call him.

"I told you he had other motives. Once you put some good pussy on a nigga, they stay hooked, and trust me, boo; I know you have that good shit because I can tell by the way Chris cherishes you. Love alone doesn't have that affect. I know because I have a crazy nigga sitting in the crib, watching the game right now." She chuckled right before she got up and went into her place. I couldn't believe him. I wanted an explanation, and so I called him twice before he answered the phone.

"Why did you follow me to my place yesterday? I saw you driving in my apartment complex just a few minutes ago! You can't be doing shit like that; I told you I have moved the fuck on!" I cursed him out, but he still acted nonchalant and lied at the same damn time.

"First of all, I don't give a damn about you moving on, and second of all, you're tripping. I wasn't over there." For the first time ever, this nigga was truly in his feelings, and I could hear it all in his voice.

"What the fuck ever. I know what you look like, and I know what your car looks like. Plus, I saw your license plate. You think I don't know that too, huh?" I asked, waiting for him to explain his lies.

"Whatever, all I'm worried about is when I'm going to see my son again," he said, and that was what I signed up for, so I had to figure it out as well.

"I will contact you when I can meet you," I answered and hung the phone up. This man was a fucking piece of work.

A few weeks later, everything was still going well with Chris. I had managed to take Jodie to see Sydney, but I would only do that while Chris was at work because I didn't know how he'd feel about it. I didn't know if he would try to strangle me or leave me, and for that reason alone, I had to keep it to myself. Dawn had asked me to babysit while she visited family in Florida, and I agreed because I loved her daughters, Amirah and Amaree, as if they were my own. She had also asked me to keep her dogs; I said yes to the Yorkie and no to the Pitbull for the sake of Jodie. I didn't want any vicious dogs around him.

Everything was going well. The girls would even help me out with the house and Jodie while their mother was away. All they had to do on their mother's end was check on the Pitbull and make sure he ate and had plenty of water, also that he was taken out of the apartment to use the restroom. On the sixth day, the girls did that, and all was well, except they took the Yorkie out at the same time. For some reason, I watched the Pitbull viciously attack and kill the Yorkie, and so they had no choice to call their mother. They were upset; the dogs were like family. Dawn had to rush back in town, cut her two-week vacation short, bury their Yorkie, and have their Pitbull put down. I had to watch Dawn fuss at her girls and curse them out, blaming them, and that was when I stepped in. Chris and I were out on the porch, enjoying a beer together, when Dawn started cursing the girls out in front of everybody.

"Please stop, Dawn! It isn't their fault; things happen, but you can't sit here and curse out these girls. You laid the responsibility on them to care for a Pitbull; they're only teenagers!" I yelled at her, trying to calm her down, as I stood up with my beer in my hand. Chris sat there on the chair right in front of the door, quiet, trying to stay out of us two women having it out.

"You can't tell me a damn thing when it comes to my kids. Hell, look at you; you have a good ass man, and yet you still sneak off to take Jodie to see his real daddy! This man has been a father to that child. He loves that baby, and you still couldn't help but go back!" she yelled out at me; everyone got quiet. There was no explaining that, no coming back from it. Chris went in the house, and shit went left from there.

"You took my son around the nigga that couldn't do right by you? What in the hell makes you think he can do right by Jodie? This is my son, and ain't nobody gonna take him from me. If you want that nigga, you go and be with him, but Jodie stays here with me! Jodie is my son, and I will take you to court and fight for him if you try to take him from me! Hell, he carries my last name, not that nigga's! I was there to watch his birth, not your ex!" He came closer to me. I thought he was about to choke the shit out of me; instead, he cried and went upstairs.

"Nothing is going on between us; I swear!" I cried and yelled out to him; he didn't give a damn. All the love he had given, all the money and time he had invested, I was sure he felt betrayed. He started doing shit he never had done before, leaving work and not coming home. At least not to me.

Chapter 24: Creeping with A Reason

Legacy

Each night I cried, not knowing where my man was. Not knowing when he was coming home and whom he was with. I felt ashamed. I felt so many things, and all I wanted at the end of the day was for him to forgive me, but I saw that wasn't happening any time soon. I started to go out, leaving him home with Jodie when he did come home on the weekends; I wanted him to get a dose of how I felt. I became selfish, fully understanding where he was coming from, but all I wanted was for him to understand also, and as the weeks turned into months, I started accepting the fact that we were falling apart. I should have known better than to put another man in the middle of my business when it came down to my relationship, especially a man that did, and still does, have feelings for me.

"Hey, Sydney. Can you meet me tonight?" I asked him, except this time was different. I didn't have Jodie with me, and I was at the club having a good time. He asked me where I was at, and I told him. He didn't hesitate to meet me there and pick me up either. We went to a hotel room, had some drinks, and smoked a few blunts together. I had never felt so guilty in my entire life, you know, leaving Chris at home with Jodie, just to spend some time with Sydney alone.

"You look like something is bothering you," he said, placing his hand on my thigh as we sat on the bed together, drinking some pineapple Cîroc.

"Well, a lot is wrong right now. Nothing is right, and it's been months. I am tired of trying to fix something that I have never dealt with, so I'm not sure where to even start." I felt hurt. I wanted to cry, but I wouldn't dare allow him to see that.

"What you need to do is leave him and get back with me, so you, Jodie, and I can be a family," he said, kissing me on my cheeks.

"That's not what I came here for. I can't sleep with you; I just needed a friend right now. I needed someone to talk to. I can't go to my family because, in their eyes, Chris is perfect, and we have the perfect relationship. They would grill me until they couldn't anymore, and I don't need everyone beating me up about the shit." I moved his hand off my thigh, but that wasn't going to stop him.

He grabbed my hand, pulled me up off the bed, and started pulling my pants down. I begged him to stop repeatedly, but he didn't. He started kissing me all on my pussy while I was standing up, right there on his knees. He bent me over and started stroking me from the back; I moaned and cried. It felt so good, being I hadn't had him in a long time, but it also felt so wrong because all I could think about was Chris and all the love we made together. He ripped my tank top and started caressing my breasts while he was fucking me from the back, shoving all of his dick inside of me, and trying damn hard to not miss a wall. When he was about to cum, I yanked away because I didn't want him Cumming inside of me. I wasn't on birth control and wasn't shit stopping me from getting pregnant. I was fertile as hell. Chris and I had a miscarriage six months before, and he was devastated. If he didn't want to kill me now, he definitely would if I came home carrying another nigga's baby.

"Why did you do that? What's the problem with me Cumming inside of you? We already share a son together?" he said, standing there with the cum in his hands. I was disgusted for a moment, at myself more than anyone else.

"You know that can't happen. Chris would be more than hurt; I couldn't have another baby by you, Sydney!" I yelled at him, pulling my panties up and grabbing his shirt because I didn't have a shirt, since he tore my tank top.

"Thank God this is a plain white tee. He won't notice hopefully. I feel like you tore my shit on purpose." I rolled my eyes, opened the room door, and left the hotel so that I could drive home.

That walk of shame was something else. I walked into the place I shared with Chris, saw him lying on the couch, holding our son while they slept, and all I could do was hurry and take a shower, hoping he wouldn't wake up and realize I had just arrived home.

That shit with Sydney and I went on for months. It was horrible until the point where Tisha found out and was furious. Sydney had come clean with her, told her he was leaving her to be back with me, and told her we shared a son together. She couldn't believe it, I guess, so she took it upon herself to call me on her own time and find out.

"I wanna find out what's going on between you and Sydney. You know we have been back together, and he loves me," she mumbled over the phone. She didn't sound like she believed what she was saying, but she expected me to believe that shit.

"That doesn't have anything to do with me. Where was the sympathy for me when he was my man? I don't have time for this shit, Tisha!" I yelled at her, about to hang up the phone on her, until she asked me that one question.

"He told me y'all have a child together... is the child his?" she asked. I could tell she didn't want to believe the truth; so how would she have benefited from me keeping it real with her anyway?

"Yes, Jodie is his son," I told her, trying not to sound proud, but hell, I was. I was proud of my child; he was the love of my life, so it didn't matter to me what Tisha felt at this point.

I could hear her crying, although she tried her best to hold it in and cover it up, and then, she asked me some shit I didn't expect her to ask.

"Can I see Jodie? You have been around Rihanna, so it's only right I be able to meet Rihanna's little brother." She sounded as if she still wanted my sympathy. I said yes anyway, knowing she didn't want to meet Jodie because he was Rihanna's little brother. She wanted to see if Jodie resembled Sydney, since it was no secret that he had super strong genes. I told her to meet me at the same McDonald's that I meet Sydney at, and no doubt, when I had got, there she was, already there with her so-called best friend, Serenity.

I put my pepper spray in my purse, just in case she wanted to act stupid because I didn't fight around my son. My job as a mother was to protect him always, and I was going to do just that.

I went inside with Jodie and sat at the table while holding him close to me on my lap. She and Serenity followed us and sat down at the same table, just observing my baby.

"Do you still love him?" she glared at me, searching for answers that Sydney wouldn't give her.

"I love him yes, but am I in love with him, Tisha? No, you and I both know I invested too much time, and I just couldn't do it anymore. I am focused on my son and my relationship with my new guy. Sydney just started being there; I didn't tell him about Jodie. I didn't want Jodie around that kind of lifestyle."

"Well, I know one thing, he obviously loves you and his son. There's no denying him; he looks just like him," she mumbled, and then, she got up, as if she was ready to leave.

"He sure does look just like him; that's his twin. I told you, Tisha, now let's go." Serenity rubbed it in as Tisha put her coat on and told us she had to use the restroom first. When she came out of the bathroom, I could tell she had been crying. She had tissue in one hand, and a piece of paper was in the other hand.

"I have something you may want," Tisha said, coming closer and trying to hand me the paper. I opened the paper and looked at it; it was a name and number.

"What is this?" I asked with a puzzled look on my face.

"That's the foster parents who have London. I thought you maybe want that. I spent so many years hating you and Sydney, but not anymore. I'm letting him go, and I don't want anything else to do with him, unless it has to do with Rihanna."

I left and went home, not sure what I was going to do with the number. I was sure that if I called, they wouldn't have let me see London, and Chris' lawyer was trying to find them, not knowing they still stayed in Charlotte. Everyone thought that they had left town after they received custody, but they never did.

When I got home, things seemed different with Chris. He was sitting on the couch, as if he wanted to talk to me.

"I just wanna know who is he? You're different; we don't sleep together much anymore. You spend extra time getting dressed up, matching your panties with your bra before you go out, and you come home late some nights and get right in the shower." I was lost; I didn't know he had been paying attention to me.

"Let's talk about where you go when you leave work and don't come home?" I asked to see what he'd say, to see if he would tell the truth or not.

"I go to my mama's house," he answered; seeming confident in the story he was telling.

"No, you don't; I call her and she tells me you're not over there when you're not here. Don't try and say your friends and brothers because I called them also." I stood there, watching his mouth drop.

"I don't cheat on you though; I never have. Sometimes, I go and sit in my car and get something to eat. I think and spend some time alone," he answered, standing up and getting in my face.

"Look, I won't stay out late anymore if you won't. We'll work on getting things back how they used to be and focus on our family. We agree to disagree." I gave him a choice. He knew that if he didn't want that, he could have walked away forever and not look back. Hell, he also knew that if he only wanted to be in Jodie's life, and nothing more, I wouldn't take that from him.

"Yes, I can do that. I just want you. You know there are a lot of women jealous of you, right? I wouldn't give a damn because you are all I need - you and Jodie. I will do whatever it takes for us to be okay. I'm in love with you. You are the love of my life, and there will never be another Legacy." He grabbed me close and kissed me. Everything that was messed up between us, we made a vow to fix it. His relationship with his family didn't get any better; I guess, sometimes you just couldn't please certain people unless you were doing what they wanted you to do, so I told my baby he had to live for him and stop worrying about what his family thought because his happiness was most important. He finished law school and got a permanent job at the office where he interned. I finally stopped worrying about missing time with my babies, got myself a job as a can, and started making decent money.

After we had been together for three years, he had finally proposed, and I said yes. We started picking out our venue and planning our wedding, and my family was excited for me.

From then on, things looked up for us. I had come clean about the things I had done because I couldn't carry that burden with me, and Chris deserved honesty. He was hurt, but he told me that people made mistakes, and he forgave me.

I got my daughter, London, back; she was eight-years old when she came home to us. She didn't know me, but she knew I was her mother. She said kids used to pick on her about being adopted because she didn't look mixed, and her foster mother was white. I was guessing that when they heard her story, they realized that she needed her birth mother more than they thought she did years ago.

We raised Jodie together and had a few more babies of our own to add to the family. I had two more boys, so we had three boys and one girl together. Joseph, Jason, Jodie, and London. London loved her brothers, and they grew closed quickly. She was calling me mom, instead of Legacy, within months of getting her back.

My father, Yankee, started coming around and started being in his grandchildren's lives. After all, that was what I wanted because there was no way we could have made up for lost times; that wass until he got arrested and went back to prison for robbing a bank. A little birdy told me that he robbed BB&T, and the loan officer was so shook that he quit and never came back.

Oh, and I heard that the social worker in charge of my case lost her job. They found out that she was taking money to hinder cases, so foster parents could adopt children that were in the system with a breeze.

Sydney, aka Skrilla, was out of the picture for good, and he became sorry anyway. When I cut things off with him, he decided that if he couldn't have me, then he wouldn't have anything to do with Jodie; but I was fine with that. I found out that Jodie wasn't his only son; he had so many kids in Charlotte that he couldn't keep count himself. I heard he was always struggling, and he never had any money because there were so many child support cases open on him. Luckily, I wasn't one of them, thanks to my supporter, lover, and best friend, Chris.

I became the happiest I had ever been in my life when I stopped being infatuated with a real nigga and fell in love with a real man. My man was happy, I was happy, and our children were healthy and happy. We moved out of that two-bedroom apartment and purchased a four-bedroom house with a white fence around it, like I always dreamed. Oh, and my wedding, let's just say it was all that I could have ever dreamed of and more, with some star guest performances. I said goodbye to being a little girl and hello to being a woman. I found out that Chris had never stepped out on me, but I was happy he had forgiven me for the things I had done.

But hey, there was a saying, 'what goes around, comes around.' Right?

The end

Text Shan to 22828 to stay up to date with new releases, sneak peeks, contest, and more...

Check your spam if you don't receive an email thanking you for signing up.

Text **SPROMANCE** to 22828 to stay up to date on new releases, plus get information on contest, sneak peeks, and more!

CPSIA information can be obtained
at www.ICGtesting.com
Printed in the USA
LVOW04s0012041016
507217LV00025B/801/P